FALLING

RALPH ZIEFF

PART ONE
FIGHT AND FLIGHT

ONE

THE FIGHT

Hank Bellakoff felt sick to his stomach as he reeled backwards, his swollen face barely recognizable through the blood and sweat. He heard his head thud on the canvas floor, and his eyes, although more than half closed, were watching the swirling merry-go-round world of the Boston Arena spinning by.

He became aware of two legs near his head, legs in black pants, grey socks, and very well-shined black Italian leather shoes.

"Four," the owner of the legs called out. "Five...Six...Seven."

At "Seven," Hank's head and vision had cleared just enough for him to make his re-entry into the Middleweight fight, now in the eighth round, that he had been in until being rudely interrupted by a leathery black blob that had mashed the left side of his nose, probably breaking it.

"Watch out for his fuckin' right hand," he had been warned, just two minutes earlier by Bubba, his manager, in his brief respite before Round 8, and yes, it was the right that smashed into his face hard enough to produce a heavy flow of disgusting metallic-tasting blood.

Hank took two wobbly steps toward the referee while clumsily trying to wipe the blood away with his gloved right hand and lifting his left enough to show he was ready to fight on.

"I'm good...I'm good," he said when the ref asked if he wanted to continue.The referee grabbed both of Hank's gloved hands, shook them enough to be able to tell whether or not he had enough strength and looking into his eyes to see if he was sufficiently functional to continue, and then backed off as the hard-charging Archie Sanborn came in for the kill. He swung wildly at Hank's head and missed. Hank lunged forward and grabbed onto the fighter, wrapping his arms around him at elbow level, nullifying all of Archie's bad intentions for almost twenty seconds...just thirty seconds more to get out of the eighth round.

By doing lots of backing up, Hank got to that rescuing clang that followed the predictable canvas thumping by twelve seconds.The thumping was always supposed to be a ten second warning that the round was almost over, but Harry Goodson, a long time Arena employee was always purposely early. Harry believed doing that was giving an edge to any home town fighter who knew about it over an out-of -towner who didn't. In this case, Hank just clinched a little longer until the bell.

In his corner, Hank learned from Bubba that as usual he hadn't listened, was not using his hands enough, and was "sleep-walking" his way through this bout... and that he was about to lose to that "old dumb fuck" Archie, who was actually two months younger than Hank, both men being an almost over the hill thirty-six.

When the bell rang for the ninth round, Bubba just about pushed Hank off the stool. Hank's face had smudges of Vaseline all over it, especially around his nose, which was still oozing a little blood. The ring doctor jumped in front of Hank with a flashlight, shined it in Hank's eyes as a cursory concussion check, looked closely at his nose and asked him if he really wanted to continue.

"He's fine, Doc, leave him alone...he's okay," Bubba yelled, and Hank nodded and mumbled, "I'm okay, Doc...lemme go."

The doctor, Iggy Luchesa, was a long time Ring Doctor with a very specialized practice that had only Mafia members as patients. "Okay, but I'm only giving you one more round at most, Hank...Are you sure you can breathe?"

Bubba declared that Hank didn't need to breathe, just punch, and told his fighter, "It's knockout or lose, Hank. Go get the bastard."

Hank dutifully stumbled back into the middle of the ring, and an almost growling Archie came charging at him as the bell sounded for Round 9. Hank got distracted for a split second, seeing the almost fully exposed breasts of the Round Card girl who was bending to get through the ropes as she left the ring, just one of those habits that never goes away. Because of the distraction, he caught a solid punch on his right shoulder, a rather harmless shot, and then, making it look as accidental as possible, punched ol' Archie a good four inches below the belt of his ugly purple satin trunks, evoking a pained howl from "the old bastard.'"

Archie crumpled down to one knee on the canvas, yelling "Chezus, Ref!" The referee bent down to talk to the fallen fighter, asking him if he needed some time to recuperate from the low blow. Archie nodded yes, and the referee told him he could have up to five minutes to do so. He then approached Hank and warned him that any other low blow would cost him two points on the judges' scorecards, and a third would result in disqualification, and loss of the fight. Hank thought to himself, "Two points ? Shit, I'm so far behind that points don't mean anything to me; I either knock him out, or lose, like Bubba said."

Archie used almost four of the five minutes allotted to a fighter recuperating from a low blow, then stood up, told the referee, "Let's go!", glaring at Hank, and the ref waved for the two men on to resume fighting. Something told Hank that an angry Archie would be out to decapitate him. He knew his burly opponent was well aware that he had purposely hit low, and nothing makes a fighter any more angry.

Hank was right. Archie came lunging at him and landed a left on his right cheek bone that hurt, but far from being the guillotine Archie wished for. Hank, anticipating the wild rush, saw in a flash that wide open "sweet spot" which was the right side of Archie's face. Summoning up every ounce of remaining strength he had, Hank landed a thundering left hook to Archie's right cheek bone and temple, and watched as his opponent crumpled to the canvassed floor with a thump, blood already oozing from the right side of his mouth, and then a glassy-eyed look up at Hank.

The referee didn't bother counting, but rather waved both of his arms from side to side that indicated the fight was over. He then waved for Doc Luchesa to get into the ring, and within a minute the ref, the Ring Doctor, and Archie's corner men were all kneeling next to the fallen fighter, one man putting a pillow under Archie's head. Hank, aware of how hard he had punched the man, watched nervously from his corner as Bubba was yelling praise and congratulations at him for the startling knockout. He saw that Iggy and his trainer were talking to Archie, but there was no real response from the still-conscious fighter.

Within minutes a stretcher was brought into the ring, Archie placed on it, and it was taken out of the Arena to a smattering of respectful applause from the still shocked crowd.

"I don't like this, Bubba," Hank told his still celebrating manager. "I think I may have killed him."

Bubba turned to look at the stretcher just as it was going out the entrance way and said, "Naw...He's a tough guy; he'll be okay."

An ominous feeling growing in Hank was telling him that for once he was right and Bubba was wrong.

TWO
HENRY BELLAKOFF

Henry Bellakoff (his parents never gave him a middle name. Hank always told people his family was too poor to afford one for him) was born on March 18, 1956, in Boston's West End neighborhood, to Lithuanian Jewish immigrant parents. He also always told people that if he was born one day earlier he would have been an Irish Catholic. Only to those who knew him best would he say that he wished he had been born three days earlier, on the Ides of March, because then just one back-stabbing would have done him in, rather than the multiple ones he had already experienced. He got no argument about that from those who knew him well. His back seemed particularly scarred from his relationships with women. There were many, and of those, quite a few had inglorious endings.

Hank, the older of two boys, with a three year younger brother, Barney Charles (the family must have had more money for giving a middle name when Barney was born) was a high energy athletic kid who was a good enough swimmer to be a life-guard at Boston's men only L Street Beach. There was a women's side behind a high wall that many a man tried to scale believing the women were nude as some of the men were (although a little stringed jock strap was supposed to be mandatory), only to find out they wore bathing suits. Every once in a while a very excited teenage boy would be running around the men's side yelling that he caught a glimpse of a naked girl.

The mandatory crotch cover for men was intermittently enforced by Bruno, a huge ex-heavyweight boxer with two cauliflower ears, a dulled mind, and a long handled feather tickler used to tickle uncovered. "packages." That was a "Get covered or else I'll bounce you out" warning from the man no one wanted to tangle with. No one ever knew how much this former New England heavyweight champion made for strolling the men's side of L Street Beach looking for naked balls to tickle, and no one really cared.

Hank also started fighting at a Boston boxing club when he was fourteen and took to the sport immediately. Between those endeavors, his job selling newspapers, and his high school studies, he was one busy boy because his father, a barber, died suddenly at age 43 while cutting someone's hair. Hank, then twelve and the older one, became the designated replacement for his father, which meant he would be the one to go out and earn enough to support his mother, his little brother,...and oh, yeah...himself. His mother, understandably bitter about being suddenly abandoned with two young boys, always found young Henry to be the best target for her anger and resentment, partly because he looked a lot like her dead husband.

Hank dropped all his odd jobs when he turned pro as a boxer at age 18. He also somehow managed to graduate high school, and with pretty good grades. He was actually a lot smarter than he ever gave himself credit for. He was fortunate to meet Bubba Dixon early in his amateur days at the boxing club, and Bubba, a pretty decent middleweight fighter in his day, taught him a lot.

The highlight of Bubba's career had been a tenth round knockout in an ABC TV Saturday afternoon semi-final bout, of Johnny Godello, a former world contender. While he was a local celebrity for a while after his TV glory, Bubba's career stalled badly because of a broken right hand and too much Jim Beam. He was never able to come back fully, and he decided to become a teacher/manager when he was given a good offer from Whitey Zackman, who owned one of the best area fight clubs.

Bubba was to become the only person in Hank's life that he ever really trusted. It seemed like all the people in the fight game, if they weren't Italian, were Jewish, just enough to convince Hank, on Bubba's advice, that he didn't need to change his name to Kid O'Halloran to be successful.

When Bubba first met the teenage Hank, he was impressed with his toughness and his smarts, and made him his number one project. The kid learned quickly, and with his natural powerful punching ability with either hand, was destined for a championship someday, Bubba believed.

When Hank turned pro, still just a kid, he got off to a flying start, knocking out his first six opponents (chosen for their ineptitude), and then won three straight decisions over some decent local fighters. Then, when a former welterweight title holder who gained enough weight to try to move up a division was looking for a relatively inexperienced middleweight, Bubba offered up Hank, but insisted that the fight be fought in Boston rather than Milwaukee, the ex-champ's home town. It was the main event in a Thanksgiving weekend promotion, and the fight stirred up a lot of interest in the Northern New England area.

"This is your first real test, kid, and I know you can beat that has-been," Bubba repeatedly told the nervous Hank.

On the night of the fight Hank, hearing the din of the big crowd that was there to watch and cheer for him, threw up in the dressing room. Bubba convinced him that puking before a big fight was a good thing, and he mentioned a few well known area athletes, but especially the great Bill Russell of the Boston Celtics, who often threw up before basketball games.

Hank also threw up again in the dressing room after being

knocked out in the fifth round by the ex-champ. Bubba was not so happy about that puking, but told Hank it was really okay that he was no longer undefeated.

"Too much pressure," he said. He also said Hank should think of the loss as a good learning experience that will lead to important improvements in his boxing skills.

Hank usually thought of such comments from his caring manager as Bubba's own brand of happy horseshit, and they usually did nothing for his mood.

"Yeah, there ya' go, in one ear and out the other," Bubba would say when he could tell Hank wasn't taking him seriously. But both men knew that when Bubba was really teaching him some important boxing stuff, like how to find that little "window" in your opponent that is open for an uppercut, the teacher/student relationship was golden. Hank continued to rise in the middleweight division rankings, to the point where he was now considered the #4 challenger for the championship. The big knockout over Archie would likely raise him to #3.

However, over these years of boxing success, Hank was taking his lumps outside the ring, with a string of broken relationships with women, most ending hurtfully for the very romantic Mister Bellakoff. Falling in love was very easy for him, and women gladly reciprocated, drawn to his self-confidence, his genuine respect for women, and his powerful boxer persona. His handsome Lithuanian looks (very fair skin, killer blue eyes, and jet black hair) just added to his aura, and Hank spent very few months in his life when he wasn't connected to someone. The women he chose were never the brassy, aggressive "bimbo" type. Women who were more subtle, intelligent, funny and yet sophisticated, were the type he would chose, and most were slender or petite.

Bubba didn't like most of Hank's girlfriends, viewing them as distractions for Hank, or competitors for his own role as the most important person in his boxer's life. The major exception to that was Beverly Ross.

Beverly was all the things Hank wanted, and none of the things Bubba feared. Both men always agreed that Hank's and Bev's three year relationship was the best ever. When the relationship ended two years ago, for reasons Bubba never understood, he was almost as heartbroken as Hank. Hank himself was devastated, and for the first time ever said he was done with relationships. That resolve lasted about three months, when he began an affair with the wife of Jack Toohey, one of the three biggest boxing promoters in New England.

Donna Toohey was a slinky, sultry, gorgeous brunette that every man who knew her lusted for. Being married to the much older but wealthy Toohey worked for her up to a point...spending yes, screwing no. She was immediately attracted to Hank, and she let him know it in every way she could without being obvious to others, especially, of course, to Jack, who was known as "that Irishman with the violent temper."

Hank eventually succumbed to Donna's pursuit one hot August night in the bushes outside the Toohey's lavish mansion, where inside Jack was doing solo schmoozing with the elite of the Boston sports scene. The encounter was both passionate and painful as both got their rear ends jabbed by sharp little branches and even sharper thorns. Luckily, the music was playing loudly enough inside for no one to hear the "Oh God!"s and "Ouch!"s" from the groping and panting couple. It was clear to both from this first encounter that it would not be their last. Three months later Donna broke it off, telling Hank that Jack was getting suspicious, and she was not prepared to risk her lavish life style nor Hank's career, or maybe even his life. While Bubba was convinced it was only her life style she really cared about, good ol' romantic Hank preferred to believe she did it to protect him.

When it hit the newspapers a few months later that Eduardo Gomez, a promising local light-heavyweight with movie star good looks, was fished out of Boston Harbor with multiple bullet holes in his once powerful torso, the area boxing community immediately covertly identified it as a Jack Toohey hit due to Eduardo's messing around with Donna Toohey. Bubba saved his "I told you so!"s, knowing Hank would just find some way to explain it that would allow him to hold on to his romantic fantasy about his relationship with the very hot Donna.

THREE

THE DRESSING ROOM

Hank sat upright on the massage table, still sweating and still bleeding, with a blood-stained white towel around his neck.Bubba was into the supply cabinet, pulling out some bandages and tape, gauze, iodine, and a large pair of scissors.

"We gotta get you ready for a trip to Boston City so someone can fix that broken pussy-sniffer of yours," Bubba told Hank.

"Christ," responded Hank, "do you always have to be so gross?" Paradoxically, at that same moment, Hank had been fantasizing his nose deeply nestled into that gorgeous Card Girl's sweet spot.

"C'mon, kid, gimme those hands. I got just about five minutes before the ambulance is ready for your ride after they get back from taking Archie over there. I've got to get those gloves off you, Jeez they're bloody, and re-tape your hands, and do a little patchwork on your honker."

"Do you really think Archie's okay, Bubba ?"

"Yeah, yeah...I told ya', he's tough as nails."

"Yeah, Bubba, but I hit him really hard, as hard as I've ever hit anyone above the neck, and he looked like shit on the mat, sort of like he was there but he wasn't."

"They'll fix him up fine at Boston City, Hank. C'mon, give me the other hand."

There was a knock on the dressing room door.

"Come in," yelled Bubba.

In strode Jack Toohey, wearing a gorgeous and obviously expensive camel overcoat draped over his shoulders...a classic big-wig outfit, both men thought silently.

"Hey Jack, did you catch my boy out there?" Bubba asked with a proud grin on his face.

"You know I did, Bubba,...Hank...and you know that's why I'm here now," Jack replied. "I think we should be looking ahead, and I've got a few big ideas for guys, but tonight I'll just say congratulations, and call me on Monday. Okay?"

"Sure, sure", said Bubba.

"Hey Jack, you hear anything about Archie at Boston City?"

"No, Hank, but I think I heard someone say they was shippin' him over to Mass General."

The dressing room got deadly silent for a minute, and then it was Hank's "Oh shit!" that eventually ended it.

"Hey, don't go into that goddamned guilty shit you always do. He wrecked your fuckin' nose, and you hit him a clean shot, so if you hurt him bad, so what!" Bubba asserted.

"Yeah, Hank," Jack added, "Don't get yourself all worked up. Think positive. Hey, look you guys, I gotta get out of here and get home. Donna is throwing another one of her big parties, you know, Hank, you been at a few of them."

"Yeah, I remember. Good night, Jack."

Bubba reiterated that he would call him on Monday, and with that, Jack left. As he headed out the dressing room door he passed by Will Sargent, the grisly veteran sports writer for the Boston Globe, who was on his way in to see Hank.

"Hi, Hank," Will began. "I'm not gonna keep you long, but I just have to ask you about...well,...Jesus, Hank you really laid out Archie Sanborn tonight, big time, and I promise you, I'm really gonna give it a big write-up for the morning paper. How were you able to come back like that after him messing you up like he did?"

"I don't know, Will, you were at ringside... What do you think?"

"Well, okay, Hank, if you're asking me, I think that low blow from you gave you plenty of time to clear your head, and I think it sort of screwed Sanborn up a little."

"Maybe so," Hank responded, with eyes searching the writer's craggy face for what else he might be thinking.

"What else?" Hank nervously asked.

"Well, Hank, to be perfectly honest, and you know I've been covering boxing for a lot of years, that low blow looked pretty much intentional to me...but hey, I could be wrong. The ref didn't call it, and that's what really counts."

"Get the fuck outta here, Will, you crazy old fuck!" Bubba ineloquently broke in.

"Bubba, shut up!" Hank retorted. "I want to know what he thinks. I asked him, for God's sake."

"Hey listen, you two. I gotta go to work to get my story ready for the morning. Bubba, Hank, listen, I'm just gonna write an accurate description of the fight, including the last couple of rounds. I'm not gonna add my personal observations, okay?"

"Yeah, fine," Hank said, more for Bubba than for himself. Bubba just grunted some unintelligible sound, and Will was gone

"That guy's a real asshole," Bubba declared.

"C'mom Bubba, you know why he said that."

"Hank, we gotta finish getting you ready; they'll be here any minute.

Bubba was right. A young ambulance worker walked in a minute later saying Mister Bellakoff's ride to Boston City was ready to go, which is what they did, riding off in the ambulance into the chilly Boston night air.

FOUR

THE HOSPITAL

As Hank and Bubba got out of the ambulance at the Boston City emergency entrance, Hank's stomach did a flip-flop, as he liked to call it when describing his love-at-first-sight to different women. Only this time it wasn't love, it was fear. Walking quickly toward him was Izzy Luchesa, the Ring Doctor. This had never happened before. He didn't think Doc was that concerned about his broken nose, a fairly common ring injury, and this flip-flop was because his mind was once again on Archie.

"Hey, Doc", Hank quickly blurted as Doc got closer, "What's up?"

"Did you hear about Archie goin' to Mass General?"

"Yeah, Doc. How's he doing?"

"Christ, I just heard the poor guy slipped into a coma. I'm headin' out there now. You wanna drive with me?"

"No way!" Bubba.said emphatically. "He hasn't even been examined yet. He can head over there after they work on his nose, but not before."

"Goddamnit, Bubba, Archie could be dying. The hell with my nose, I'm going right now. Yeah, Doc, I'll ride with you."

Hank and Doc Luchesa rushed out of Boston City and into the doctor's black limousine, leaving an infuriated Bubba behind.

When they got to the Mass General, one of the most respected hospitals in the world, both men jumped out of the back seat, rushing toward the emergency entrance, leaving Doc's chauffeur to take care of the limousine.

Once inside, Doc found out quickly where Archie was, and they headed for the Critical Care unit. As they approached Archie's room, they were confronted by at least a half-dozen sports writers, all of them beseeching Hank to tell them how he was feeling about the plight of his vanquished foe.

"I feel horrible," Hank declared to all. "How the hell do you think I'm feeling!"

The group included Eddie Weston, Archie's manager, who just glared at Hank for a minute, then turned and went back into the room. When Hank and Doc Luchesa started to enter the room, Eddie was at the door, saying "Just you, Doc. Not him."

Hank backed off immediately, not really that surprised by Eddie's reaction to him. He walked slowly, head down, into the small visitors' room, which he quickly regretted. He was immediately recognized as that monster who may have murdered Uncle, Cousin, friend, Brother, Son, ex-husband and Father Archie, who pitifully lay in a state of near death just a few rooms away. And here was the man with the gloved gun who shot him down, with the balls to enter the grief-filled family's waiting room.

"Yeah, you bastard, get the fuck outa here!"1 one woman yelled at Hank, which he immediately did. He ended up sitting on the floor a few doors down from Archie's room room, with his back against the wall. And that is exactly how Hank was feeling, his back was against the wall. He thought to himself that no good can possibly.come from tonight

FIVE

CHELSEA MEMORIAL PARK AND BUBBA

Hank stayed pretty far back from the gathering that surrounded Archie's coffin. He stood amongst a few large trees, wearing dark sun glasses that covered his black eyes and bridged over his bandaged nose. He could make out a few of the priest's words, and could tell when people were crying. He himself felt numb during these past five days, not going to the Wake, of course, and having to answer the same questions from the media over and over again.

"Yes, my nose got badly busted but it will heal."

"How do you think I feel about Archie's dying? I feel sick to my stomach about it. It's not what I wanted. I really liked Archie, and now there's nothing I can do about it. But I do intend to help those kids as much as I can."

"The low blow? I don't clearly remember it, I was so busted up when I did it, I can't actually tell you for sure."

"Will I box again? I don't know. I love boxing, but I don't know if I can ever feel good again hitting guys, or even putting on gloves again. I just don't know, but if I had to decide now, I would tell you I'm done fighting."

The papers had stories ranging from give Hank a break, boxing is a violent sport and all fighters know the risk they take, to wanting Hank charged with at least involuntary manslaughter, His lawyer, Anthony Salvano, told him not to worry, that things will cool down in a few weeks, and that he will take good care of him if he needed a defense attorney.

In the meantime, there was a meeting scheduled for Monday in the Massachusetts State Boxing Commissioner's office for a hearing at 10:00 a.m.

Hank had decided to go back to Chelsea Memorial today, by himself, or with Bubba if he wanted to go. He stopped by the Club, found Bubba, and saw that his manager was truly upset about Archie.

"C'mon, Bub let's go to the cemetery together."

Hank surprisingly got no argument from Bubba, and soon the two men were standing together at the newly shoveled grave: Bubba with his wear-stained Red Sox baseball cap in his hands, head bowed, and Hank, again surprised by what seemed to be some deep emotion in the man who rarely expressed feelings, to him or to anyone.

Harold "Bubba" Dixon. He hated the name Harold, especially the way his Brooklyn born mother would yell it out her kitchen window when she wanted him to come in from playing street football, or hockey, or basketball in the driveway of their Somerville home. "Haaaruled' she would yell, with that nasal twang that she also used when saying she needed her morning "corefee"...The nickname "Bubba" was popular in the sports world, so when a friend of his started calling him that, he liked it, and let it stick.

Now the six-foot-one former boxer was standing next to the top fighter that he managed, and he, Harold Dixon, was doing something he hardly ever did in his whole life. He was crying. Yes, the kid Harold who never cried when his father would beat him with a tree branch, or a leather strap, or his fists. The beatings were often combined with his father yelling at him that he was a bum, a stupid goddamn worthless bum who would never amount to anything, but Harold never cried, never wanting his father to see his weakness and vulnerability.

Now, here he was, tears streaming down his cheeks, and his fighter, his boxing student for God's sake, was watching him cry, and then even asked Bubba about it, a type of question Bubba would never even attempt to answer

"Hey, Bub, what's happenin' man? I didn't know you cared about Archie at all."

Bubba surprised even himself by replying "I feel so bad that he died. I was always sayin' how tough he was, because to me bein' tough was what it was all about. That's what I learned from my old man. Bein' tough was the only thing that crummy bastard cared about. I would have liked to be married like Archie, have kids, not just be a boxer. But I lived my life always focused on bein' tough."

"Hey, man, you sound like you're the one who's dead and buried. You can change all that. From now on, you can be who you really are, a great manager, a great guy, and a real person who can be tough and also be kind and caring, and not some make believe tough guy."

Bubba gave no reply, because he really didn't know what to say, but he heard Hank loud and clear, and was letting those words flow through his inner being. He also didn't look at Hank because his tears still embarrassed him a little. And then, about a minute later, Bubba turned toward Hank, grabbed him and gave him a hug, the first such embrace ever in their relationship. Until this moment, they had both relied on guy-type contact, either a handshake, or a light shoulder punch.

The two men went back to the Club, with little conversation during the ride. However, once inside and in Bubba's closed door office, the two began to talk about the upcoming meeting with the Commissioner. Hank began by telling Bubba how god-awful scared he was of that meeting, and Bubba- no, the new Bubba- said that he was also scared of it, but knew that he and Hank would receive the benefit of both having a totally clean record over the years.

When Bubba added himself to the prospect of punishment at the hands of the Commissioner, it was the first time Hank acknowledged to himself that his manager could be in trouble also.

"Hey listen, Bub, no way am I gonna let them drag you into this. I will swear to them that you had absolutely nothing to do with my bad decision, and you know that's the truth. It's not your style, Bubba, it never has been, and it never will be, and the Commissioner knows that."

"Yeah, so Hank, it's never been your style either, so what the hell are we worrying about?"

"My hands killed Archie, and I can't deny that. I know I'm not likely to get charged with a felony like Involuntary Manslaughter or some kind of assault charge because of the law's definition of boxing, and the known risk taken by both fighters when they enter the ring. But the one complicating fact that has me scared as far as my boxing career goes is that the low blow I started the sequence off with was not an accident, and it was that intentional foul that set up the rest of the horror show."

"I think you need to get away from here until Monday," Bubba advised. "Go get laid. Maybe that will get your mind off all of this."

"Naw, that won't help with this, Bub", Hank said as he slowly started walking toward the door. He paused for a moment, and then said, "Hey, Bub, you don't happen to know the first name of that Round Card girl from the other night, do you?"

SIX

THE ROUND CARD GIRL

Hank left the club feeling a rush of anxiety, having just verbalized for the first time his fear about losing his whole career in boxing. He had loved boxing since he was a young teenager who had just lost his father and who needed a family, so to speak, of people who supported him and appreciated him, something his mother was not doing at all. Barney did express appreciation to his big brother, but that had not been helping Hank, because Barney appreciated Hank for what he was doing for him, not because of who Hank was as a person. In the Club and especially in Bubba Dixon, Hank found what he needed.

Now Hank still had the support he needed from Bubba and his inner circle of friends, but the rest of the world was on the verge of condemning him and wanting his head, as that fairy tale about Alice had so well described. Now it was the Commissioner of Massachusetts Boxing rather than a crazy queen, but the end result could be the same.

Hank stopped off at the Shamrock and got a straight double of Jack Daniels. As he was sipping that mellow Tennessee sour mash nectar with every drop charcoal filtered, he beckoned Chucky, the drop dead handsome bartender. That good looking twenty-three year old probably knew every girl who ever came into the bar, a popular watering hole for the boxing crowd.

"Hey, Chucky, my old buddy, do you know most of the Arena card girls who come in here?"

"Hey, Hank, I didn't know we was buddies." Chucky was so handsome that Hank was sure women would easily excuse him for his bad grammar.

"No listen, man, do you know them? You must, a handsome dude like you."

Chucky blushed a little and then admitted that he did know a bunch of them, them numbering about nine or ten, and that from his description, Hank had to be thinking about Molly Riley.

"Ah, a nice Jewish girl," Hank joked, which got a lovely dimpled chuckle from Chucky. God, the girls must really love this guy, Hank enviously thought to himself. He thanked Chucky (who had no idea how to "get in touch" with Molly Riley), gulped down the rest of his mellow Daniels tranquilizer juice, and left the Shamrock.

He debated whether or not to go searching for beautiful Molly or just head for home, when a loud car honk got his attention, and helped him immediately decide what to do next.

It was Donna Toohey in her cream colored Lincoln Town Car, beckoning to him. Hank dutifully obeyed, and as he approached her car he heard Donna saying, "I thought I might find you at the Shamrock. I'm really sorry about what happened, and I know Jack is too.".

"Yeah, thanks." Hank replied in a soft, flat voice.

"I've missed you, Hank...a lot."

"Not THAT much," Hank replied, "not with that Latin lover you had that Jack turned into a piece of Swiss cheese."

"What are you talking about?"

"Eduardo Ricardo Montalban Gomez," Hank teased, alluding to the hot Latino Hollywood idol.

"What? Eduardo? You asshole, Hank! I know everyone's buzzing about how that rich slut, Donna Toohey, had a big romance with him, and that Jack found out and had him murdered. Neither of those things are true. I slept with that narcissistic bozo one time. I missed you, and I couldn't resist the Latin charm. One time! That's all it took me to be able to tell between a man who loves women, and a man who loves only himself and being loved by women. Being with that jerk that one time made me miss you all the more, Hank. I mean it."

Hank sidestepped his real feelings of wanting to grab, hug, and kiss Donna, instead going with his logical, rational curiosity.

"So, then who got pissed off enough to ventilate jerky Eduardo?".

"I have no idea," Donna replied, "and neither does Jack, who by the way doesn't know I laid Eduardo, so please be discrete."

"Will do," Hank answered, but his mind was oddly struggling with a piece of Donna's information that just didn't feel right, and was gnawing at him. If Jack didn't want Eduardo dead, then who did, and why? Not being clear on why he even cared about why and by whom Gomez got murdered, because hell, he didn't really know the guy. Hank pushed it out of his mind and continued to engage with Donna. The Round Card girl was now nowhere in his thoughts.

"Want to get one at the Sham?"

"I would love to, but I've got a husband at home who's probably right about now starting to make up a fantastic batch of Spaghetti Caruso for our dinner with Doc Luchesa. It's Doc's favorite, and it really is delicious, and Jack will be really upset with me if I'm late."

"What the hell is Spaghetti Caruso?" Hank asked.

"Oh, honey!"

Her calling him that caught them both by surprise, and got Donna to pause and look into those damned sexy blue eyes. "Okay, one drink only."

"Good! Now what is Spaghetti Caruso?"

"It's a spaghetti dish named after the opera singer for whom it was created, by a chef who loved opera. Caruso loved fried chicken liver, with this scrumptious red sauce that I think had a lot of Marsala wine in it. Do you like chicken livers?"

"Well, when I was a kid I had an old aunt who used to chop up chicken livers with some hard boiled eggs, and some chicken fat, fried onions and garlic and turn it into this delicious stuff that was like a pate. Some Jewish delis have it and call it chopped liver. I used to love that stuff and a lot of other things she used to make, like cabbage soup and potato pancakes, and blintzes, which were like crepes or raviolis filled with cheese or meat."

"Hank, how come you never took me to a Jewish deli. Was it because I'm not Jewish?"

"Donna, for God's sake! No, it wasn't because you weren't Jewish. It was because, like when did we ever get to just go out like normal people and not slink around hoping not to be seen? There are a lot of things we never got to do, Donna, and you know why."

Donna got quiet, got out of the car, and she and Hank went into the Shamrock for one drink. They grabbed a table where Handsome Boy couldn't hear their conversation. The two sat silently for a few minutes, and it soon became clear to each what the other was feeling, because they were both feeling the same thing.

"It's probably a good thing you've got Mr. Caruso waiting for you at home, because I swear, Donna, if we sit here much longer I'm going to have to jump your bones!"

They both giggled at Hank's use of that worn-out expression, but Donna let him know he would only be able to do that to her if she hadn't already done it to him. They wisely finished their drinks quickly and, knowing Handsome Boy was watching them, said a polite "goodbye, good to see you" to each other and left separately, Donna first.

The way Hank was now feeling, having seen Donna, he felt it would not be a good time for Molly-hunting, and told himself that the Round Card girl would have to wait until the next round.

SEVEN

WILL SARGENT AND THE NEXT ROUND

Hank was feeling a lot better after his encounter with Donna, knowing that not only did he still have a thing for her, but she still had a thing for him. He got into his car and headed for home. As he drove past the Club, he noticed Will Sargent going in the door. Hank pulled over and waited to see if Will would come out within the next few minutes. He figured he was the central figure in what would certainly have to be the biggest story for Will to be covering, and assumed Will was looking for him.

Just as he thought, Will exited the Club within a matter of moments, probably in there just long enough to say hello to Bubba. He spotted Hank in his parked car across the street from the Club door, and immediately called out to him that he was just the person he was looking for.and within a minute was seated next to Hank in the front passenger seat.

"Glad I caught you, Hank. I'm writing a story that will be in tomorrow's paper, and I wanted to give you a heads-up on it. As I told you, I've got to walk a thin line between needing to call 'em like I see 'em and at the same time not fry your ass, because I really like you and I don't think you deserve that."

"So what's that mean?" Hank asked.

"Well, I do say I thought that foul looked more like a strategy than an accident, but I go on to say things like that do happen in boxing, and that Archie set up both of you for a possible disaster by not controlling his anger and foolishly rushing at you, wide open for that big shot.from you. The shot you gave him was clean, and just very powerful. I also mention that you've had a totally clean record your whole career.and that his big punch had messed you up quite a bit, and you might not have been thinking very lucidly at the time you fouled him. I mention your preliminary meeting on Monday with Charlie Schumacher, and that's about it."

"Preliminary meeting?"

"Yeah, oh Jeez, that's right, you've never gone through this process before. First you and Bubba will meet with just the Commissioner. I think Archie's people have met with Charlie already. After that he develops a report for the Commission members, they hash it over, reach a consensus about what they believe should happen regarding the matter, and then meet with you for a resolution."

"Tell me honestly, Will, how scared should I be?"

"Well, I'd love to say don't worry, but there is a big risk, Hank. You know there are two possible ways of looking at this, and the more negative one would definitely carry some consequences for your license. I don't see any criminal charges, but for the Commission to do nothing would make for a bad public image for the sport. I think a one or two year suspension is most likely."

"Can I fight outside of Massachusetts if they do that?"

"Yeah, if you can get licensed in another state, but that might be difficult to get, with the notoriety and all."

"So c'mon, Will, I'm really screwed, aren't I?"

"I don't know, kid. I would tell you if I thought I really knew, but these things are so damned unpredictable."

Will Sargent spent the next twenty minutes or so hashing over the fight with Hank, occasionally stopping to write short-hand notes to himself on a medium sized legal pad of lined yellow paper. He thanked the fighter for helping with his story, and said he would do the best he could for Hank with it. He wished Hank well, and left. Hank just sat there for a while, staring into space, and lost in his own fearful thoughts.

Once again, he started driving toward home, when as he passed the small Bay State Junior College campus, he saw her: Molly the Round Card girl. She was sitting with four other girls roughly her age, which he estimated to be about twenty- two or three.She looked beautiful, as she had the night of the fight, but now Hank felt virtually nothing in the way of real interest or desire. Was it that he saw Donna, or that he was too bummed out about the fight to be interested, (although he sure had lusted for Donna)? Or maybe both?

Hank sat in his car for a moment or two, decided he was definitely TKO'd in this possible next round with Molly, and drove off for home.

He never ever thought about her again.

EIGHT

COMMISSIONER CHARLES SCHUMACHER, AND OLD MISTER POTTER

It was seven a.m. when Hank's alarm went off as he lay in bed, newly awake. He immediately felt sick to his stomach. The realization hit him immediately that in three hours he would be sitting in the Commissioner's office, probably wetting his pants. He felt like he might be able to do his best Bill Russell imitation, but that feeling passed, and he didn't.

He knew he needed to shower and dress, eat some breakfast if he could, go to the Club to pick up Bubba, and bring the newspaper so he and Bub could read Will's article together. Hank had read the first one the day after the fight (twice) and felt it was neutral, as he had been hoping Will would make it. He wanted to have time to check out Bubba's recollections of it all, but Will had suggested they not really work at coming up with the exact same story. He felt Schumacher might see that as a symptom of guilt. He also advised Hank not to bring a lawyer to the preliminary meeting, because that, too, might look like an admission of guilt. But he also said don't even think about going without one to the full Commission meeting.

Hank peed, brushed his teeth, drank some instant coffee, took a shower, put on a charcoal grey suit, white shirt, and silvery grey tie, and headed off for the Club. The breakfast idea he just couldn't handle. He wondered for a moment whether Bill Russell ever ate before Celtics games.

Hank stopped at Smiley's Smoke Shop to buy the morning paper, and had a hard time not peeking at the sports section in the back. When he got to the Club, Bubba was sitting in his office, also dressed uncharacteristically in a black suit (Bubba had once told him he only got dressed up for funerals), and the only white shirt he owned, open at the neck.

"Hi, kid. Did you sleep okay?" When Hank answered that no, he didn't, Bubba responded with, "Well, that makes two of us. Jeez, Hank, I just don't know what to make of this meeting.with Schumacher. The only time I ever met him was at the Club one day that he stopped in with a bunch of other people to show them around. He said he'd heard only good things about the Club and also about me, and that was it. He seemed like an okay guy, but today still has me very nervous."

"Yeah, me too Bubba, but listen, I've got today's paper, and Will interviewed me yesterday for an article today, so I thought we could read it together."

"Yeah, sounds good, but Hank, there's somethin' important I've got to talk to you about."

"Can it wait until later today ? We really need to focus on the meeting."

Bubba looked somewhat dismayed, but said, "Sure, whatever you say."

Will's article surprised both Hank and Bubba with how supportive it was of the idea that in spite of the tragic outcome, the situation called for leniency in light of Hank's character, and the fact that the low blow was not directly related to Archie's death.

The two men smiled at each other, Bubba saying, "I like it, I like it a lot," and Hank saying,"Man, I'm a little surprised, but I'll take it!"

"C'mon", said Hank, "we don't want to be late for the meeting."

As the two rose to leave, Bubba's phone rang. "Should I take it or let it go?"

"Might as well take it, Bub."

It was Donna on the phone, hoping Hank was still there because she needed to talk to him.

"Hank, Honey, I've got to tell you what Doc Luchesa said last night."

"Did he like the Spaghetti Caruso ?"

"He loved it, and I love you, and listen. He said with a look that he knew what he was talking about, that he believes you will make out fine at the meeting with Schumacher."

"Okay, great", Hank replied, thinking more about Donna's "I love you" and brushing off Doc's comment as kind and supportive."I gotta go. I can't be late for the meeting. Thanks, Donna. I'll call you after."

Soon, Hank and Bubba were parking a few doors down from the State House Annex, where Commissioner Charles Prescott.Schumacher had his office.

Charlie Schumacher grew up in Belmont, a rather affluent suburb of Boston. The son of a Harvard grad father financier and a Bryn Mawr mother high school teacher. As an only child, he grew up in the world of the "privileged class",or as Bubba always said, the "privileged ass." And that indeed appeared to fit Charles S. Schumacher quite well. His office was decorated with gorgeous cherry furniture, including a very elaborate desk and lots of expensive looking boxing-related oil paintings.

"Sit down, guys, I'm glad to get this chance to meet with you."

His greeting carried with it the inference that the meeting was voluntary, which, of course, it wasn't.

"Hank, I'm Charlie Schumacher, and I know we've never met before, although I've followed your career very closely. I'm sure you know you're considered one of our State's very best fighters. Your record is excellent, and I'm sorry it's been marked by the Sanborn tragedy, the reason we're meeting today."

"Yeah, well me, too, Commissioner."

"Please, call me Charlie."

While puzzled by the friendly feeling of the encounter so far, Hank wasn't about to question it, and simply replied with, "Okay, Charlie."

Schumacher then swiveled his desk chair so he could open a desk drawer, and took out what looked like an expensive amber glass and bronze humidor. From it he pulled out three large cigars with beautiful red and gold seal wrappers, saying,"Honduras", and offered one to Hank and one to Bubba. Both men accepted the offer, and the Commissioner quickly lit his own, and tossed his Tiffany lighter to Hank, who lit his own, and then passed it to Bubba who said, "No thanks, I'm gonna save this beauty for tonight."

Hank's reaction to his first puff was to cough, of course, him not being a smoker of anything, never mind cigars. Well, actually he had shared a joint with Donna on several wildly passionate occasions in the past.

And then it happened. Commissioner Charles Schumacher leaned back in his chair, putting his feet up on his desk, clasping his hands behind his head, and puffing on his Honduran King in the classic posture of a confident and powerful man.

"Look, Hank, let's cut to the chase.You know why you're here, and we're going to figure out a deal that will leave you and people reasonably satisfied that the Commission did its job."

Schumacher's use of the word "deal' jolted Hank. A deal? The Commissioner is going to offer him a deal? That idea took things a long way from where Hank thought they would be. In fact, they took things so far off that Hank wasn't himself now, but rather he was now Jimmy Stewart, the actor, in the Bedford Falls office of old Henry F. Potter in a famous scene from "It's A Wonderful Life", many people's all time favorite Christmas movie. In the scene, George Bailey (Stewart's character) is being courted and offered a devious self-serving deal by snarky, slimy, sinister Mr. Potter, the richest man in town. Potter (Lionel Barrymore) has given Bailey a big cigar and is passing off a totally selfish deal as an offering of help and kindness.

George Bailey suddenly realizes the scam that's going on, stands up and throws the cigar away, and tells old man Potter that there is not and will never be a deal between them, and that he'll be just fine without any help from Potter.That image took over Hank's being to the point where Charlie Schumacher now looked exactly like Lionel Barrymore.

He rose from his chair, snuffed out his cigar, and said just like George Bailey did, "Now you listen here, Charlie"...and that was as far as he got. Realizing he was about to blast off on the Commissioner of Boxing, who really did hold his future in his hands, Hank froze up for a moment and then finished his sentence with, "...are you saying you think I came here to work out a sneaky deal with you?". It was the best he could come up with, and it proved to be good enough for the Commissioner not to label him insane or reckless.

"Hank, man, sit down, will you? Jesus, I wasn't saying that at all. I'm saying I am offering YOU a deal, and I think it's a good one for everyone. And why didn' you tell me you don't like cigars?"

"Well, Charlie, you're the Commissioner, a very powerful person, and very important to my future career in boxing, so I wasn't comfortable saying "No" to you."

Bubba did a double take, hearing Hank just say something that couldn't have come from the Hank he knew so well.

Schumacher responded, "Hey, look, Hank, I always need to hear honest straight talk from you, because that's what you're getting from me, okay?"

Hank thought to himself "Yeah, sure, Charlie...sure, straight talk!" but to the Commissioner, he replied only with, "Okay."

For the rest of the meeting, Charlie rolled out the plan, and Hank accepted all of it as "okay." Both he and Bubba would express curiosity to each other on the way back to the Club as to why he might have left Bubba totally out of the conversation. Hank then additionally told Bubba he was really confused about how what was supposed to be a hearing turned into being a deal proposal. Someone had obviously already done some serious talking with Schumacher before he met with them. Hank's mind tried but failed at figuring out who and why.

"So Hank, if you're so upset about all that, why did you tell Charlie you accepted his deal?"

"Great question, Bubba my friend, great question. If I answer it, do you promise not to ever talk about any of this to anyone other than me, and I do mean anyone?:"

Bubba swore to Hank he never would tell anyone anything. Hank believed Bubba, and proceeded to explain his decision in very simple but ominous terms.

" I said yes, Bubba, because my gut tells me that if I were to say no, our lives might be in grave danger."

"C'mon, Kid, stop shittin' me, will you? You make it sound like a TV show or somethin'. Who would be out to get us, huh?"

"I really don't know, Bub, but we damn well better figure some of this out pretty damn quick."

NINE

DONNA TOOHEY

The deal Schumacher offered Hank was so good for him that he immediately started worrying about why he was getting off so easy, just as Doc Luchesa had told Donna and Jack. He was even more worried about what would happen to him if he somehow failed to fulfill his end of the bargain. He knew all too well that in the boxing game, at least in Boston, if you screwed around with a deal, you could end up looking like a piece of Swiss cheese, like poor Eduardo Gomez.

Hank had never taken a dive in his life, and knew, deep down, he never would. But he knew that guys who would make those kinds of deals were playing a dangerous game with very dangerous people. They were also often hard up for money, which Hank wasn't. He had been doing well enough with his fights, and was typically careful with his money, so while he didn't have a lot (a championship would change all that), he never had to worry about whether he had enough.

The conditions of the deal were straightforward enough, but Hank's suspiciousness persisted. The Commission would simply put out a press release that would discuss the seriousness and sadness surrounding this tragic ring accident, reprimand Hank in the mildest terms possible, and place him on probation for two years. During the probationary period, if Hank were involved in any kind of "flagrant foul" incident when fighting, whether accidental or not, his State license would be suspended for a year, or permanently if more than one incident occurs.

In exchange for this mild response, Hank had to agree not to fight for the next six months out of respect for the grieving Sanborns, and for Archie himself. He also had to plan a fight for a title shot at the current champion Willie Watson before the year was out, that fight to be against the current number 10 ranked Middleweight, Anthony Brandisi. To sign for a fight with Brandisi would involve his by-passing six or seven fighters ranked higher than number 10, with Hank's own ranking probably being number 2 after his destruction of Archie. Those other guys would be screaming about Brandisi not deserving to be in a title elimination fight, and Hank and Bubba would have to play up the "toughness" of Brandisi, and his "heart of a warrior," to justify the jump. As far as he knew, that was it, all that Hank had to do to get the Commission's light response to the Sanborn fight.

Hank had readily agreed to the deal, but at some level he knew this was not at all as clean and simple as it looked. Bubba didn't seem comfortable with it either...

"Kid, what if they decide they want this Brandisi guy to win when you and him fight?"

"Great question, Bub, and that worries me, too."

"Would you take a dive for whatever sons of bitches are arranging this thing?"

"You mean this,"Oh, this 'let's be kind to Bellakoff' thing? You know Bub, I don't know what I would do. Taking a dive just isn't in me, but, I also don't want to die, and I don't want you to, either."

"Listen, Kid, there's something I really need to talk to you about. It's about the fight, somethin' I should have told you about that night, but I just couldn't. I felt really bad about what I had done, but after the fight, things just started moving so fast that I just hung on to it.

Then I was starting to tell you this morning, but Donna's call came in, and I..."

Hank interrupted. "C'mon Bubba, out with it. What did you do?"

Bubba shifted in his chair, looking at the floor, visibly upset.

"Cheez, Hank, I feel like shit about this. I've always given you my best, and you've done the same. And you are always honest and fair with me: that's why I feel so bad about this."

"Okay, okay, Bubba, I get the point, you're sorry, very sorry. About WHAT? Who did you murder?"

"C'mon, Kid, you know it's nothin' like that."

"Of course I do, Bub, but are you ever going to tell me what you did do?"

Bubba rubbed his burly right hand over his face, took a deep breath, and finally blurted out, "I nearly got you killed that night, either killed, or your career ruined."

"Bub, what are you talking about? What night?"

"The fight, Kid, the fight." Bubba paused, took another deep breath, and continued. "Remember when you were busted up pretty bad, your nose busted, lots of blood...what a mess you were?"

"Yeah", Hank responded. "Sure I do. What about it?"

"Remember when Doc Luchesa came over to see if you could continue, and then he decided you could?"

"Were you surprised when he let you fight?"

"A little,...yeah."

"Do you remember what I was doin' at that time? Christ, Hank, I was pushing him and you to keep it goin'. I was scared shitless you were hurt real bad, and everything in me wanted to stop it and protect you from more damage."

"So why did you push to keep it going? I do remember you said to Doc that I didn't need to breathe, just punch. That was a little unusual, for you to say something like that."

"Of course it was, Kid,...I love you like a son."

"Yeah, well you and I both know Bubba that there are

37

father/manager type guys who would never let their kid quit, and watch them get beat to a pulp, whether for money, pride, or both."

"Money, Kid, that's what I did it for. Money!"

Again Bubba paused, and then confessed to Hank that he had put down ten thousand dollars that he had tucked away over the years as a deposit on a thirty thousand dollar bet on Hank to knock out Archie Sanborn. The problem with that, Bubba explained, was that he didn't have the other twenty thousand unless Hank knocked out Archie. Hank was surprised Bubba had bet not just on him beating Archie, but on a knockout. Bubba explained he was convinced Archie didn't have a lot of gas left in his tank because of having too many fights over the years.

"You know, Kid, I brought you along slow so you wouldn't burn out young, like Archie."

"Yeah, Bub, I know you did, and I appreciate that. So since I did knock him out, what's the problem with money?"

Bubba's answer gave Hank a cold chill, and a confirmation of his fears about the contract with Schumacher.

"Hank, you gotta listen to me. There's some real bad people behind the scenes in Boston boxing now, just like in New York and Philly. After that round when you got busted up good, some guy I never saw before came up to me and warned me that they would expect immediate payment if you lost, or I would end up looking a lot worse than you. That's when I pushed Doc to let you fight. I am so sorry, Hank. You know there was a chance of Archie killing you, or your career, if he played his cards right. Hank, I think there's like a big mob influence involved in this, so even the Commission deal scares me."

"Yeah", Hank replied, "and if I hadn't messed him up with a dirty punch, he might have. You think I don't feel terrible about THAT?"

What Hank didn't say was that he fully shared Bubba's fears of the mob...the largely invisible mob. He felt an immediate need for some warmth and nurturing, and called Donna. Yes, she would meet him in a half hour at his place. Giving Bubba a hug and telling him all is forgiven, that they should both be watching their backs, and that he would try to find out more from Donna, Hank took off for home.

When Donna arrived about five minutes after Hank, a discussion about the mob underbelly of Boston boxing was not high on their agenda. They were out of their clothes in record time, and re-established their obviously enduring intimate connection. Lying next to each other in bed, Donna's head resting on Hank's left shoulder, was a frequent setting for deep discussions between the two in their brief past, and now was definitely the right time for such a talk.

"Okay, so listen Hank, the time away from each other helped me get really clear with myself about you. I love you, very much, and I now know I want to be with you over the long haul. I really regret not being able to say that back when we broke up. I think Jack's life style bullshit was blinding me to my real feelings. I know it might take you a while to trust me again, but I want *us,* Hank, more than anything".

Hank pulled her on top of him and kissed Donna passionately, this woman who was now clearly giving herself to him more completely than ever. He surprised himself with how much more than ever he reciprocated that intense love and desire. The two just held each other for a few minutes, and then Donna made the minor adjustments needed to get Hank to be totally inside her, and they proceeded to experience the bliss of total intimate connection. Afterwards, they spent a while lying facing each other but without speaking. Their focus on each other was all that was needed, no talk required.

They eventually ran out to Asian Palace, the little Chinese restaurant, hardly a palace, across the street from Hank's apartment, and took out two orders of Pork Lo Mein and one Chicken Egg Foo Yong. In their bag, when they were back in Hank's small kitchen, Donna found two fortune cookies, and she insisted they had to open them before the two hungry lovers attacked their food...She ended up wishing she hadn't.

Hers was, " *The wisest person is always the cautious one*" and Hank's was, " *You will prevail over obstacles ahead.*"

"Great, Babe, why don't we just take the easy route and develop a suicide pact right now!" Hank jested without any enthusiasm.

Donna responded with a very simple and wise, "Let's eat."

They ended their time together with one more sexual interlude, once again declaring deep love for each other, and Donna heading home to Jack, who had promised that tonight they would go out, yes, for Chinese food. Hank wished her good luck with that one.

TEN

JACK AND DONNA TOOHEY

The China Pagoda was not very busy on this Monday night, and Jack and Donna Toohey were seated opposite each other at a very small but private table in the back of the dining room. They were just digging in to their Moo Shu Pork when Donna asked Jack about rumors people have been telling her about mob involvement behind the scenes in Boston's boxing world.

"Oh for Christ's sake, Honey, is that what you want to talk about on our night out?"

"Jack, Honey, we have lots of nights out, and you know it."

"Yeah, well it's not a great time or setting to have any kind of discussion like that, and besides, people have been rumoring about stuff like that since the 1930's."

Donna was struck by how neither of Jack's two deflections denied the rumors. She had long suspected Jack kept many secrets from her, especially related to where some of his big money came from, and who he hung out with business-wise.

She knew his secrets had to be of a less than savory nature, and she often flashed back to that famous scene in the "Godfather" movie when Diane Keaton asks her husband, Al Pacino, a.k.a. Michael

Corleone, who is now the Godfather, if he is involved in criminal enterprises and murder, and he simply looks at her and says "No, no I'm not," and she breathes a sigh of relief, smiles, hugs him, and the movie ends, until the later sequel, that is.

"That dumb or naive I am not," Donna thought to herself.

They continued with their meal, which included shrimp in that characteristically Boston extra dark lobster sauce. Jack always said "Chinese lobster sauce is like everything else in life, because there ain't even a friggin' whiff of lobster in it. That was Jack, Donna's beloved husband, at his most cynical. Most of the time he played "Mister Happy", trying to gloss over all of life's struggles and disappointments with money, and things, many things. Donna's world was full of wonderful shiny things, and she was good at playing "Mrs. Happy." But now, she realized there was only one thing she really wanted, and that was Hank.

When she and Jack first met nine years ago, she was a bubbly young thing, and engaged to Larry Alexis, All-State quarterback and her high school steady her junior and senior years. Larry was an extremely handsome and sociable guy who was Senior Class President, and every girl at school considered her incredibly lucky to land a hot catch like Larry. Larry was actually envied by all the guys because Donna herself was so good looking.

Donna and Larry were doing well, although Donna sometimes felt he was either too nice, or too superficial, or both. They were starting to put together wedding plans for the following spring, when, enter Jack Toohey. Donna found herself immediately drawn to this flashy, self-confident, twice-married older man, who wanted for nothing materially. She had met him at the wedding of Larry's cousin Nina, Jack being a close friend of the groom's father, the owner of The Dancing Fisherman Greek restaurant in Boston North End. Jack was alone, asked her to dance three times, and pitched hard and fast to the point where she agreed to meet him for lunch the next day.

Things took off quickly from there, and Larry's jealousy became her excuse for ending their engagement. She and Jack married six months later. Jack, who had been married and divorced twice, his wives' infidelities the reasons he always gave, had one daughter with his second wife, but he never had a relationship with her, and now with her in her early twenties, he had no idea where she lived or whether he might even have a grandchild. Donna thought the daughter issue bothered him more than he would ever talk about, but that was on the long list of problems that Jack glossed over with those ubiquitous shiny things.

After dinner, on the short ride home, not a word was spoken, and when Jack said he was tired and went to bed two hours earlier than usual, Donna started to worry. Was it her questions about the mob? Or was it that she was emanating something, feelings, or even a smell, about Hank? She panicked for a moment, wanted to call Hank but didn't, and eventually followed Jack to bed.

The next morning, Donna made bacon and scrambled eggs with cheddar and sweet red pepper, Jack's favorite. As he drank his coffee after polishing off the meal, she made another attempt to get him to open up about the ominous presence of the mob in their area. He was a little more forthcoming than he had been in the restaurant, and Donna learned that a hood named Big Tony Ferrante was the visible head man, but that everyone knew there was someone else at the very top, someone who chose to keep their identity hidden, an invisible ruthless "top dog" that everyone feared.

Donna asked what Big Tony was involved in, and Jack just said, " Oh, he's just a typical tough guy, an enforcer, taking orders from Mr. Invisible, and involved directly in any big money-making enterprises."

"Like boxing?", Donna asked.

"Like boxing", Jack replied. Donna felt an immediate anxiety chill.

"So what does Big Tony do as an enforcer?"

Jack responded, "Thanks for breakfast honey," and left the breakfast nook, going into their lavish living room, and turning on the TV to ESPN's Sports Center.

Donna imagined that Diane Keaton at that point would probably start making a batch of chocolate chip cookies for Al Pacino. She, on the other hand, was determined to follow Jack into the living room and repeat her questions about Big Tony's enforcer job description. Again, Jack deflected, this time asking her where this new-found interest in the mob's role in Boston boxing.was coming from. He knew she really enjoyed the three Hank Bellakoff fights they went to, with her becoming a very animated and vocal member of the local crowd cheering for Hank, their hometown rising star fighter.

Donna couldn't think of what to tell Jack, so she got up from the sofa in a huff, and stormed back into the kitchen, muttering something about how frustrating he was when it came to communicating. Jack settled back into Sports Center, while Donna put breakfast dishes and frying pan into the dish washer. She was wanting to see Hank so badly that she started thinking about an excuse she could use for spending the afternoon out.

"Jack, honey, I think I'm, going to head downtown to do some shopping", she was saying to her husband, whose response was simply "Okay, Honey." He was glad to get rid of her for a while, with all her incessant questions about things she shouldn't know.

Within an hour she and Hank were, let's say, wrapped up closely with each other at Chez Bellakoff, their own little hideaway. They were almost lost in the throes of passion, but neither one was ever letting go of that underlying fear that if they were ever discovered, they both, or at least he, would end up looking like a slice of imported Swiss cheese (the holes often being bigger in imported than in domestic Swiss cheeses).

"Listen, Donna, I know you're afraid and so am I. We don't even know who or what we're afraid of, but we're both getting bad enough vibes that we've got to start developing a plan...a sure-fire survival plan, and right now I think that means getting out of Boston,...of Massachusetts", he added, knowing he would never be able to fight again in the Bay State, home of Rocky Marciano and Jack Sharkey... and Bill Russell. He added the greatest professional basketball player of the Twentieth Century to the two heavyweight world champions because he was feeling very nauseous right now, out of fear he could lose Donna permanently as a result of this discussion.

Hank was expecting her to give him her usual reasons for concluding that she could never leave Massachusetts because she didn't want to leave Jack. How shocked he was by her real response, which was:

"Hank, I love you so much, and I will do whatever you want, and go wherever you go, if you want me to."

Hank encircled her arms with his in the gentlest of bear hugs, and they rolled off the bed onto the floor, holding that embrace for many minutes, no words spoken, but silence interrupted by the sounds of two people crying softly, crying together.

———

Jack Toohey was sitting in his living room in his chestnut colored leather recliner, and dialing the phone number of someone he had hoped he would never have to call. He heard four rings, and then a "Yeh?"

"It's Jack, Jack Toohey."

ELEVEN

BUBBA

Hank and Donna spent the rest of what little time they had left reveling in their new-found sense of mutual commitment. As she was leaving, there was no big kiss, but rather a long and passionately felt hug. Slightly wet-eyed, she flashed a big smile, and left.

Hank was feeling like Gene Kelly doing his iconic "Singing In The Rain", dance, bursting with energy, gleeful with joy, and madly in love.

He drank a small glass of green Gatorade (sex can rob you of electrolytes, he thought with a smile) and then headed for the Club, needing to have a talk with Bubba. It was dark out now, and the New England night air had a real bite to it. Hank raised the collar of his dark brown Air Force type short leather jacket to shield the back of his neck against the gradually strengthening breeze.

When he pulled up and parked right in front of the Club, Hank quickly entered the surprisingly dark building. There were usually people staying late, and the few who closed it up at night, like Bubba, sometimes decided to leave a few on to discourage would-be bad guys from breaking in.

But tonight there were no lights, and the Club had a slightly dark and ominous feel to it as he began walking through the place, calling out Bubba's name, getting no response. When he got to Bubba's office, there was no light on, which would not be unusual, Bubba being so cautious about electricity bills getting too big. However, seeing Bubba's wooden swivel chair tipped over and the dark green pillow he used on it on the floor beside it, gave Hank a very cold chill, and the beginnings of a panic reaction. Bubba would never leave things that way in his office, and Hank knew that as well as he knew Bubba, or at least thought he knew Bubba.

"Bubba! Hey Bub, where the hell are you?", he called out, yelling now, and fearful. "Bubba?"

Hank started running, now knowing there was something wrong, something bad going on,...bad for Bubba.

"Bubba! Bubba!!" Hank was now just about screaming the name of his manager and best buddy, and while there were no sounds in the Club, the silence was deafening for Hank, and he screamed his Bub's name two more times. With no response, he ran in and out of both bathrooms and both locker rooms and then, heart pounding, made a mad rush past the small steam room and into the weight lifting area.

Up against the wall across from him was Bubba, sitting on the floor with his head in a down position, bleeding from several locations above the shoulders. Straddled across his legs was a 300 pound barbell that clearly had him pinned in that spot.

"Bub, Jesus, Bub,...Oh god, Bubba," he called out as he rushed to Bubba's side. He cradled that messed up bleeding head in his arms for a minute or two, seeing that most of the blood was coming from his nose and mouth, but also that while unconscious, he was definitely breathing.

"Bub, who did this to you? What happened?", he asked his beloved but still unconscious manager, not thinking clearly enough to see the absurdity in that.

Hank continued to sit with Bubba for a few more minutes, until the silence was broken by a familiar voice.

"Hey, you jerk-off, where are you? Where the hell are you hiding, Bubba? I'm in a rush and I have to be at the Lowell P.A.L. boxing tournament very soon. In fact, schmuck, I'm late already. Where the hell...Oh shit, Hank, what's happened?"

When Ira Reitlin, the Club's official sign and poster maker saw the the bloody head resting on Hank's shoulder, he rudely vomited on the floor mat beside him before Hank could start a reply

"Sorry!" he blurted out, and then threw in, "No, don't tell me, I don't wanna know, I just got to get out of here. Sorry Hank...Sorry, Bubba" as he raced toward the entrance.

"Ira, call 911...Ira,for fuck's sake,...IRA!"

Apparently Ira heard Hank, because a Boston City Ambulance and two cops were there in five minutes. Hank rode with the cops, following the ambulance right up to the emergency entrance. Soon, Hank was sitting in empty waiting room, not at all like the crowded one at the Mass general that fateful night. Here, Hank had a chance to calm down, sit back, and get control over his breathing enough to relax his incredibly tense, tight body. God, he wished Donna was with him. She could help him get rid of any pain he's ever had through her nurturing love, but right now, it would have to be calming himself. His attempts to do so were often being interrupted by his morbid thoughts about losing Bubba.

Hank was almost nodding off when a tall, lean doctor approached him and asked if was a relative of Bubba's. Hank explained their relationship, and the doctor decided it was good enough to let him talk. He told Hank Bubba had lost a lot of blood (most of it appearing on Hank's clothes), was very weak, and was now sleeping. He suggested Hank leave and come back in the morning, but Hank stated his intentions were to hang close until Bubba could talk. No life threatening injuries but lots of internal damage, was the rest of what Hank learned from the doctor, who then wished Hank good luck and moved on to his next patient.

When Hank went outside for some fresh air, he told himself he was certain that the attack on Bubba was a sign of grave danger for him and Donna, and he seemed closer than ever to being able to grab Donna and flee Boston, flee Massachusetts, and maybe even flee the East Coast. He sat on a bench close to the hospital entrance, holding his bowed, aching head with his hands, but bolted upright at the sound of a familiar female voice saying, "Hello, Hank."

He immediately saw that it was Beverly Ross, more beautiful than ever.

"Bev?" he responded. "Wow,...I mean, like what are you doing here?" Hank quickly recognized that his attempts to calm himself down were now hopeless.

"Same thing you are, Hank, I'm here to visit Bub. I heard about how viciously he was attacked, and I just had to get over here to see him. He is such a dear man, and I still do care a lot about him."

Hank proceeded to give her the doctor's update on Bubba's condition, and then suggested they grab some coffee in the hospital cafeteria, which they did.

"Are you okay sitting here with me, Hank? You really don"t have to be polite, and just..."

"No, Bev, this is fine. I'm fine.", which proved to be the biggest lie he had told in a long time.

TWELVE
HANK AND BEV REDUX

Hank and Bev sat in silence for a few minutes, feeling awkward, uncomfortable, or both. Bev eventually broke the silence.

"So, how has your life been since we parted, Hank?"

"You read the papers, don't you?"

"Yeah, of course I do, but I meant apart from all that boxing drama."

"Lately, I haven't been having much of a life apart from that."

Bev took a sip of her black coffee, eyes raised to make contact with Hank's, and a slight smile creasing her face as she finished swallowing the sip.

"That's odd", she said, because I've been hearing that that Lithuanian Jew boxer was in love, again!"

Hank cracked a smile of his own and quipped, "Talking like that, Ms. Ross, it's a good thing you're Jewish."

"Well, is it true?" Her eyes were now piercing as she continued her eye contact with her former lover.

"Don't believe everything you hear, Bev."

"Fine, but is it true? C'mon boy, don't be answering a fair question with a fortune cookie response. Is it true?"

Tired of playing this silly game, he said, "Yes, it's true."

"Wonderful!", Bev exclaimed. "Who's the lucky girl, Hank?"

"Can't answer that," Hank responded, taking a full drink from his coffee. "How about you?"

"How about what about me?"

"Men...a new guy in your life?" Hank was aware of just having asked a question to which he really didn't want an answer.

"No, Hank, not really." Bev then excused herself and headed to a ladies' room.

Hank, while still feeling a few old tugs of desire for this intelligent and beautiful woman he once was very deeply connected to, was aware of a certain level of unease with her, maybe a product of their break-up, but additionally a brand new feeling, suspicious, which he never experienced with Bev in the past. Why? He wasn't sure,...he just was.

After Bev returned from the bathroom, they chatted on for about ten more minutes until Bev rose from her cafeteria chair, saying, "Hey, look, Hank, this has been nice, catching up with each other, but I've got a few really important errands I have to do in town, so I better go up to see Bub now."

Her use of that nickname for Bubba she had of course picked up from Hank, and he was flooded for a few moments by visual memories of the three of them, "The Three Amigos", as they called themselves, on so many occasions: laughing, drinking, playing, being silly,..."Bye, Hank", Bev interjected into Hank's mental photo album.

"Huh? Oh, yeah...Hey, it has been nice, Bev. You take care, now."

Bev headed off toward the hospital elevators, and Hank decided to head for the Shamrock. After a few beers there, he returned to Mass General and Bubba's room. He was still sleeping, and this time, when a nurse suggested he go home and come back in the morning, he took the advice.

When he got back to his apartment, which was actually the right half of a wood framed duplex in a quiet residential neighborhood, he breathed a big sigh of relief. Between the assault on Bubba and a crappy encounter with Bev, Hank was glad to be home...until, that is, he went into his bathroom to gargle himself to a Listerine clean mouth. The taste of the cafeteria's burnt coffee and of a sour meeting with Bev left him needing that fresh, clean, tingling feeling in his verbal orifice, as he liked to call it, believing that with some guys you can't tell the difference between the two. With women? Three was just too many for any man to figure out.

He entered the bathroom, turned on the light, and there, scrawled in red magic marker on his cabinet mirror was *"Be A Good Boy or Be a Dead Boy "*

Hank mumbled an "Oh shit!" to himself as he backed up to the bathroom doorway. This, he knew, was not good. Not only had he just received a death threat, probably from the same sweethearts who almost murdered Bubba, but also, they were inside his apartment! If ever he was ready to grab Donna and get out of town fast, now was the time. he still needed to see Bubba, but after that, it was bye-bye

THIRTEEN

BUBBA'S CONFESSION

On his way to the hospital the next morning, Hank stopped at the Club, using the spare key Bubba had once given him, to check on things, which he did, and also to try to reach Donna and plan their escape. The first time he called, praying she, not Jack or Gertrude, their maid, would answer, no one answered, and when the answering machine clicked on, he quickly hung up. He tried again ten minutes later, and this time Donna picked up.

"Donna, my love, it's time for us to get out of Boston. It's,D-Day, it's here, now...Meet me tonight with a packed bag."

He explained it all to her, and when she heard the mirror part, she broke in and said, "Hank, honey, I'll meet you at your place at five, ready to travel. For me it will have to be, Sorry, but I have to 'Hit The Road, Jack."

They both giggled at the irony in the song title, said another "I love you" to each other, and hung up.

When Hank got to Bubba's room at Mass General, he was shocked to find no Bubba, the room vacated, and the "Dixon" sign removed. In a panic, he grabbed the first person outfitted in white or blue he could find, a very pretty, young Latino janitorial woman who told him Bubba was being transferred to a post-surgical unit.

"What surgery?" This was the first Hank had heard that word regarding Bubba.

"You'll have to ask a nurse," replied Elena, the name block typed on the I.D. placard she wore, dangling from her neck.

"Okay, I will." Hank found his heart beat racing, a low level panic beginning to set in.He needed to see Bubba, but he also had to leave town in a hurry after Donna got to his apartment that evening. Bubba in surgery? What the hell does that mean?

Hank stopped the first nurse he saw, who told him she'd have to check at the nursing station. She quickly returned with the information. Bubba had just had his broken jaw wired shut to aid the healing process, and would be wired for six weeks. He was currently still "under" in a post-op room, and would eventually be moved to Room 302 in the hospital's Tobin wing. Visitors would be allowed after 2:00 p.m.

Hank, somewhat rattled by this news, thanked the nurse and turned to leave, but then struck by a pang of fear, turned back and called out to the nurse, "Will he be able to talk?"

"No," she replied, "not for six weeks, but he'll have plenty of paper and pens so he can communicate with notes."

Hank stood frozen in place, able to say nothing, as the nurse moved on down the corridor. After a minute or two, he headed down to the cafeteria, grabbed some coffee and a doughnut, and sat by himself, head often in hands, for several hours.

At around noon time he was getting hungry enough to grab some lunch right there at the Café Mass General, famous for their egg salad sandwiches and fish sticks with carrots and pees. He chose a salami and cheese on rye, a bag of chips, and a Tab, read a newspaper for a while (the Globe sports section made no mention of him or Archie, which was good, he thought...maybe this whole mess will just go away), and then restlessly went to hunt for Bubba's new room.

Because he was early, Hank thought he would likely find Bubba's

room still empty, but he was wrong. There, sitting up and leaning
back on pillows, was good old Bubba Dixon himself, looking pretty
wide awake, but with his face puffed up and looking like he had just
been hit with a baseball bat. He waved hello to Hank as he entered
the room, and Hank took a chair over to the bed and sat. He noticed
Bubba's bedside hospital table had three or four medium sized note
pads and a small bunch of Mass General purple plastic ball point
pens.

"How are you feeling, Bub?"j Hank asked.

Bubba scrawled *"Like shit"* on his pad.

"You look it, my friend, you look it," Hank replied, with a facial
expression that conveyed both humor and concern. "Can you breathe
okay?"

"Not so good, but as long as my nose is clear, I'm okay."

"Bub, you've got to tell me what happened."

"It's the mob, Hank...You know that."

"But I ended up winning the fight, so what's their beef with you ?"

Bubba hesitated for a minute. His face, despite all the swelling
that distorted it, showed a mix of sadness and shame.

"C'mon, Bub, what happened?"

"I lied to you about the fight with Archie."

"What about the fight?"

" It's because you won that they are angry."

"I'm not following you, Bub." Hank was beginning to wonder if
Bubba was confused from his post operation medications, or even a
head injury.

Bubba paused for several minutes, looking down at his pad, then
glanced up at Hank briefly before starting to write, with a few tears in
his eyes that looked almost slit-like because of the swelling.

"I am so sorry, Hank, I never meant to get you into my mess."

"Bubba, for God's sake stop with the apologies! What happened?"

*"I pushed for you to go back in because I thought Archie was
gonna' finish you off."*

"What?!! You wanted me to lose, and also get more beat up?"

"Hank, I love you, kid, but I needed you to lose."

"You bet on me to lose? To Archie? Are you shittin' me?"

"I wish I was. I was being forced to get you to take a dive which would mean big money for them, and after you would wipe out Archie out in a rematch, you'd the get a shot at a top contender, and I would finally be off the hook with them."

Bubba dropped his pen on the bed and lay back, eyes closed, exhausted and riddled with shame. Hank read the two page note twice, his mind grappling with the content, that left him still confused for a few minutes, until he grabbed hold of the problem. There was something missing from Bubba's explanation.

"Bubba, what's this 'hook' you're referring to?"

Bubba closed his eyes as he took in as deep a breath as he could, turned toward Hank, and opened his eyes. Hank could see immediately that Bubba's eyes were quickly welling up with tears.

"Bubba, what is it you haven't told me? Please, Bub, tell me. It's all okay, whatever it is. You know I love you, man."

Bubba reached for his pen and started writing, never looking up as he wrote, and clearly struggling emotionally.

"You know my famous fight on TV with Godello? I won that fight and got a big name around Boston for a while, but it was all for shit, Hank. I was supposed to take a dive for Godello so he would be able to get a comeback fight with the Champ for lots of money. I couldn't handle it, got really pissed off at the things that smart-ass was saying to me in clinches, and finally I just decked the bastard in the 10th. Ever since then, I've gotten constant reminders over the years from the honchos that I owed them big time. You know the rest."

Bubba, now even more exhausted from writing this multi-note fifteen year old confessional just plopped back into his pillows, and Hank could tell from his little murmurs and slight shaking of his body, that Bubba was crying.

"Listen, Bub, as far as I'm concerned, you are still my number one man, a great friend, and one of the few people in this world I've ever trusted. I love you, man, but I have to say goodbye, old buddy. I have to screw out of Boston right away...tonight. I don't know if I'll ever be coming back, but I will never forget you and all the fun times we had, and all the good things you did for me."

Hank got up, leaned over Bubba and planted a kiss on the big guy's forehead. He turned and headed out toward the corridor, unable to turn for one last goodbye wave, because he himself was now fighting back big tears. Just as he got out the door, he heard some loud grunts coming from Bubba, and when he turned, he saw that Bubba was waving him back, almost in an agitated state. He went back to the bed and waited while Bubba wrote one final note, folded it closed, and handed it to Hank.

He then waved for Hank to go, which he did.

Hank didn't open the note and read it until he got to the elevators. The note simply said, *"You can't trust Bev, or Doc, or Jack, or Donna."*

The first three names were no huge surprise, but Donna? Why Donna? Hank thought about it for a moment and came up with two reasons why the warning about Donna wasn't one he should worry about. The first was that Bubba never trusted Donna much because she was married to that sleaze Jack, and then even more so after she later dumped Hank to stay with Jack.

Hank got his mind back into going home, finding that Donna will either be there early or arrive at the agreed upon five o'clock, and then taking off tonight for a new life with her, somewhere far away where no one will ever find them. By the time he got to his car and started it up, he was smiling, for the first time in quite a while.

FOURTEEN

FLEE BY NIGHT

W hen Hank arrived home, after making sure no one had been there who shouldn't have been, he then focused on the fact that someone he hoped would be there wasn't. It was now 5:15 p.m., and there was no Donna. Because she had a key to his place, he assumed she would let herself in and wait for him. Because it wasn't like her to be late for anything, he immediately started worrying that something could be going wrong, but stopped worrying when the only recording on his answering machine was from that lovely lady herself. Calmed by her voice, he listened to her message :

"Hi, baby, it's me. I'm running late, so I won't be there by five, but I'll come as soon as I can, so don't worry. Just stay in your apartment until I get there. Love ya' and see you soon."

Hank walked over to his kitchen table and sat down. It was good to hear her voice, and that her message was reassuring, but something about it was gnawing at him. He poured himself a Scotch and water, something he didn't do very often (beer being his usual drink of choice) and went into his living room and sat on his sofa. After a few healthy sips of his Cutty and water helped him relax a little and clear his thoughts, he ran Donna's message through his mind, and hit a couple of snags along the way. The less troubling one was her saying she was running late without explaining why, not her usual way of communicating, but especially now, with dangers lurking.

The one that was gripping him now was when she said he should stay in his apartment until she got there. Why would she say that? She has a key and could get in even if he went out for a while, and it just wasn't something she would ever tell him to do. Her typical message might tell him to relax, he's worrying too much, go out for some fresh air, or go to the Sham for a drink. For her to tell him to stay in and wait until she got there, just didn't feel right to him, and he needed to make sense out of that.

Hank took an extra large sip of his drink, leaned back against the soft pillows of his mushroom colored sofa, and raised the obvious question, why would she give him this curious instruction. When his mind quickly shifted gears to Bubba's final note, an image of Donna's name jumped out at him as if it was a neon sign.

"Oh holy shit!" he uttered out loud, and he now found himself locked in between two different answers, neither one of them good. Either Jack had found out about Donna's cheating and her plan to run, which means he was standing next to her, directing her call, with no good intentions involved, or, Donna was double-crossing him, again with no good intentions.

Hank gulped down the rest of his drink and headed outside. He had a feeling people with bad intentions were already heading his way. He started to head for his car, but stopped short, turned and ran across the street to his neighbor's house diagonally one house to the right of his. He knew he needed to stay around long enough to see who would come to his place. Maybe he was being paranoid, and beautiful loving Donna would show up as planned.

He rang the bell of the small brick ranch house, and Susie Kandler, his horny school teacher neighbor opened the door and exclaimed, "Hank, oh my goodness, what are you doing here, and do please come in!"

Susie had been chasing after him the whole three years they had been neighbors, and while Susie was a bright and very pretty Fourth Grade teacher, Hank was always focused on Bev, or Donna, and never let Susie get close.

"Hi, Susie, I'm really sorry to barge in like this,..."

"Not to worry", Susie interrupted, with as close as she could get to a seductive smile."Come sit on my new sofa, Hank, and can I get you a drink?"

Here she was, being far too obvious and pushy as usual, driven by her mad crush on her very nice man, boxer neighbor.

"Susie, thanks. What I really need right now is to sit on this great sofa, but I also need to turn and watch my apartment for a short while. I need to see who might be coming to visit that I do not want to see."

The sofa was conveniently located under the living room bay window that offered a perfect view of the wood frame duplex in which his apartment was the right half, Barry and Claire Imhoff occupying the left.

"Oh, yeah, sure, Hank...that's fine. What about that drink?"

Susie was secretly embarrassed because Hank was talking about using her sofa in a way she sometimes did when she wanted to see what the women were like who might be visiting him. She wondered if the unwanted visitor might be a woman, or an angry husband.

"Okay, Susie. How about some ice water ?"

"Sure, but nothing more serious, like I have gin and vodka...?"

"No, thanks, Susie, just water will be fine."

Susie brought him a tall glass of water with several large ice cubes in it, and Hank thanked her as he took a big swallow of the water, becoming aware of just how thirsty he really was. Fear is a great de-humidifier, he thought as he drank more. As Susie got up to get Hank a refill, a black Lincoln pulled up in front of his apartment.

"Hank, is that your unwanted company?" Susie asked innocently.

"Susie, don't talk, just get down so they won't see you."

She did as he said, crouching down on the sofa knees first, just the way Hank was, and peering out just enough over the top of the sofa back to see Hank's place. Two rather large and tough looking men in suits and ties got out, quietly closed the doors of the car, went up the stairs and into his apartment through the door he had purposely left unlocked. They came back out about five minutes later, and one knocked on the Imhoffs' door. Barry came to the door, shook his head "no" in response to whatever question he was asked. Not satisfied, the man pushed Barry back into his apartment, and the other man joined in. Hank hoped they wouldn't hurt his two kind neighbors, both retired phone company employees, with three kids and five grand kids.

The two came back out in just a couple of minutes, looked across the street, which got Hank and Susie to crouch lower, and a minute later they heard the welcome sound of car doors and the departure of what Hank thought of as the Hoodmobile. He was positive these were the two guys who nearly beat Bubba to death.

"So who were those guys?" Susie nervously inquired.

"Just a couple of mob types. They won't come back, but in case they do, either don't open your door, or just tell them you don't really know me."

"That, Hank, would not be a lie," she said with a slight smile. "Will you stay for a while?"

"Hey, thanks for letting me use your sofa, and for that refreshing ice water, but when I leave here now, you're going to see me take off after I pack a bag, driving as fast as I can out of Boston, and maybe never coming back."

"I'm sorry to hear that, Hank. I think you know I really like you...am very attracted to you, ...and oh hell, let me give you my phone number in case you need somebody here to do something for you."

She gave him a slip of paper with her name and number on it, and Hank, feeling a warm gratitude toward her gave her a quick hug, just long enough for her to plant a kiss on the side of his neck.

He ran out to his apartment, stuffed as much as he could into his largest duffel bag, decided not to take time to check out the Imhoffs, assuming they were probably fine, hopped into his car, and took off, speeding to god knows where. Before long, it was dark.

By the time he got to where the Mass Pike split off and the route to Manhattan unfolded as an option, he chose that. New York was one of his favorite places, having gone there many times with Bubba either to watch major fights or to fight on big time under cards. It would also now be a great place to hide for a day or two while he figured out where he would go next.

He stopped for gas and food in Connecticut, and soon was crossing the good old George Washington Bridge. His goal now was to get lost in the vastness of Manhattan, not very hard to do. His radio was playing "La Bamba," and he was actually feeling happy for a short while, singing along with Ritchie Valens, believing he was successfully escaping.

FIFTEEN

BAGELS, LOX, AND PLANNING

It was almost 11:00 a.m. when Hank woke up in the small, cheap, hopefully hard to find Easy Stay Motel on East 32rd Street. He had fallen asleep without even taking his clothes off when he got to his room, he was so exhausted from the non-stop emotional turmoil of the day. He knew he had a lot of planning to do, but he also knew he was starving, having had only two steamed hot dogs at the Connecticut gas station for dinner.

He by-passed the creepy looking elevator of this five story motel, and bounded down the stairs from his fourth floor room, through the tiny lobby, and out onto 33rd Street. He walked a few minutes to the corner of 3rd Avenue, and spotted a real Jewish deli across the Avenue. He made a mad dash across the street and was soon dining on a fantastic bagel, lox, onion and cream cheese sandwich so much better than anything he could get in Boston. Our Lithuanian Jewish Ritchie Valens wannabe was so ecstatic about this culinary masterpiece that he bought a second one to bring back to his room.

When he got into his room, he sat on the hard sofa near the 21 inch TV with paper and pen, jotting down some questions he needed to sort out, answer, and turn into decisions about what came next. He noticed everything he wrote involved "where should I go" type issues, not anything about the biggest question he had before him, what went down with Donna.

He wrestled with both possibilities, that she was forced to set him up by somebody, probably Jack, or she just simply set him up and double-crossed him. After a while, he let it go, realizing that at this point his decision had to be the same: never go back to Boston. If she set him up, good riddance to still another devious woman, and if Jack and the mob controlled her, she could never be his life partner, anyway. Besides, that's the bed she made for herself, twice, and she'd just have to lay in it... and without him.

He took a break, turned on TV, and went and rescued his second bagel and lox sandwich that was screaming at him from inside the little fridge near the drip coffee maker, "Come get me, come get me, come eat me."

As he ripped through that delectable sandwich, watching a noontime Manhattan news program, his mind kept wandering, first to the U.S. map he and Donna once spent a whole evening working with to try to find a place to live they would both like, and then to Donna herself...silky smooth, warm and nurturing, always smelled like a soft, powdery flower garden, and always a heavenly and spiritual journey when inside her. Why would she double-cross him? She seemed to really love him a lot, and had no love for Jack. Or, was she just a clever little actress, scheming to...to...to get what? What would she gain if I knuckled under to the mob ? "Oh, screw it !", Hank yelled to his empty room, and pulled out the U.S. map out of his bag.

Two hours later, Hank had a U.S. map with about fifteen circles drawn around areas of interest. He saw he was already a half-hour past check-out time, and was sure he didn't want to stay in the same place two nights in a row, so he grabbed his bag, put the map in it, and headed down to the seedy little lobby. He gave his key to the Pakistani guy behind the desk, and went to his car, parked in a small open lot on 33rd Street.

He debated staying in Manhattan another night, having seen that there was a WBC Cruiserweight championship fight that night at good old MSG, Ricky Melendez taking on the champ, Azeko Mfugane. He knew it could be a great fight, but reminded himself that the last places he should ever decide to be would be those connected in any way to boxing.

So, instead he filled up on gas again and had two more steamed hot dogs. Most gas station stores seemed to have them now...crunchy steaming hot dogs, soft white buns, mustard onion and relish...what else could a man want!

He decided to drive to the north and west for a while, and soon found himself on a super smooth highway heading for Buffalo. In Buffalo, he again headed for a small motel on the outskirts of the city. This time it was "The Sleepy Hollow," a one level ten room beauty. After checking the place for crawly varmints, he stretched out on his bed, and fell asleep watching an old "Hill Street Blues" rerun, woke up nine hours later, with sunlight streaming in from around his drawn window shades.

After his non-negotiable pee, he called the desk, and asked the sleepy-voiced woman who answered where the closest place was for a good breakfast. She told him Honey Dew Donuts was the only place she knew, and that was just around the corner next to a gas station. Hank whimsically raised the question for himself as to whether or not eating meals next to gas pumps could be toxic.

He took his map and pen to the Honey Dew, and after two hours, four large coffees, and three large cinnamon buns (it's good he wasn't in training for a fight, he mused), he felt not much closer to developing a destination. Maybe that's what he needed to do, just keep playing by the seat of his pants until he found a place that felt right.

As Hank approached his current home, the Sleepy Hollow Motel, his mind flashed back to The Parker House, The New York Hilton, and Caesar's Palace, reminders of what a big hit his life style had already taken. Hiding in a grungy motel in Buffalo! He wanted to add "just temporarily" to these reflections, but he was really unsure if that was true. When he turned in his key to the nearly toothless sleepy-voiced woman at the front desk, he felt even worse.

It felt good leaving New York State, and in some way, safer. He soon found himself in Euclid, Ohio, and with the need to choose at least a direction to drive in from there, he chose south and west. He thought Columbus would be a reasonable place to stay for the night.

After about a half-hour driving toward Columbus, Hank slowed down, pulled off the road into a small rest area, motor still running. He realized it was still early, he was very wide awake, probably a caffeine buzz, and that he would feel better driving all night, or most of it, to some place much further from Boston than he was now.He got back on the road, stopped to get gas and two more steamed hot dogs, and took off in a south-westerly direction for parts unknown.

" No more planning," he thought to himself. Planning was actually Donna's thing, not his. All he wanted right now was miles, lots of miles, and in between bites of a fabulous steamed hot dog, Hank was singing "La Bamba"

SIXTEEN

PLACES, AND TERRY

Over the next few days, Hank went through hundreds of cities and small towns in Kentucky, Tennessee, Arkansas, and Oklahoma with no experience of feeling that here could be my new home, something he kept hoping for. One night in West Texas, just outside of Marfa, while sitting over a plate of barbecued chicken and baked beans, he tried reviewing all the decent locations he had gone through, to figure out why they weren't connecting for him. He began to realize that the one thing they all had in common was that even though he was now a long way from home, none of these places felt far enough away from Boston and its mob of bad guys.

He pulled out his map, saw that he and Donna had once circled San Diego, a place that now looked very enticing, given that it was about as far away from Boston as one could get. That will definitely be it, he felt, relieved that he finally had his destination decided. I will be a permanent resident of San Diego, with the best climate in the country, home of the Padres, the Chargers, and the Clippers, and not a big location for boxing, which is good if you're hiding out from boxing gamblers and hoods... great seafood and Tex-Mex, close to

Baja, Mexico, with beautiful beaches and no one tickling your testes...What else could anyone ask for!

He motioned to his waitress that he was ready for his check. She was a very pretty young Chicano woman with a warm innocent smile who's answer shocked him when he asked where he might find an inexpensive nearby motel he could crash in for the night. He had been driving all day, the roads not well lighted at night, and felt it best to pack it in.

"I have maybe a much better idea about where you could stay tonight."

When Hank looked interested, she continued.

"See her over there, the one with the blond hair pulled back ? That's Terry. She's the owner, and my friend, and she's been watching you ever since you came in."

The waitress, who's name tag said her name was Tina, lowered her voice, and leaned closer to Hank, saying softly but with emotional accentuation, "She says you are hot...so hot, she gets wet looking at you, and she said to me, 'Tina, I would do anything to get in bed with that man.' So, Mister, if you looking for the nearest good place to crash tonight, you're looking at her."

And Hank, indeed, was looking at her, being several shades of pink himself from Terry's extreme endorsement of his sex appeal, and also becoming extremely aware of hers. She was a real looker, with deep set light green eyes, high cheekbones, sensuously full lips, and a body that exuded the visual potential of incredible passion. He smiled at her, and she walked toward his table as Tina backed away.

"Hi,I'm Terry."

"Hello, Terry, I'm Hank."

"Where you from, Hank ?"

"Rhode Island," he lied, not wanting anyone to connect him with Boston...ever.

"Well, you've certainly come a long way."

Hank, who was now fully prepared to flirt back, retorted, "Yes, Ma'am, I sure have."

Terry laughed after a few seconds delay, and sat down across from him, saying, "From the second you came in, Henry...Is that your full name?"

"Yes, and can I assume Theresa is yours ?"

"Yes, Henry, honey, and how about our using each other's proper first name tonight? I'm all for anything that will make the night last longer."

This time it was Hank who broke into a laugh, and simply said, "Theresa, you've got it!"

Hank had to sit for several hours until Terry could close up her modest "Mountain Kitchen" restaurant. He realized he was acting like a damned high school kid with her, but it was fun, and he was having trouble remembering the last time he had fun. Certainly, there had been none since the fight with Archie.

Terry's place was a very small white wood frame bungalow with dark green trim. Inside it was tastefully but not elaborately appointed, and the bedroom was hallmarked by a lovely queen-sized brass bed, which got many hours of passion dancing that night from Hank and Terry, most of the creative energy provided by the latter. In the morning, when Terry got up to make coffee and call Tina to ask her to open up the Kitchen, Hank was still asleep, and both snoring and smiling, or at least it looked that way to Terry. When Hank did eventually wake up for the coffee Terry placed near his nose, the first thing he said was that she almost got him thinking about staying in West Texas. As they embraced, almost spilling the coffee, Terry asked, "Almost?"

Hank explained to her as best he could, why he had to move on, not willing to give her details about why, and certainly nothing about his San Diego destination. She was very disappointed, just a little hurt, but did offer him a "return ticket" with no expiration date.They made what felt to both like genuine love-making as differentiated from passionate gymnastic combat.

They said nothing to each other as he got dressed, gave her a hug, allowed her to stick a piece of paper in his pocket, and left: next stop

New Mexico. The paper had Terry's address and phone numbers on it, and the words, "I'll always want you."

So now he had two slips of paper with the phone numbers of women on them. Maybe, he thought, I could start collecting these. At the same time, he was aware that one of them, Terry's, meant much more to him than the other one that Susie had given him. Nevertheless, Susie's was the one he would soon be using.

PART TWO
DESCENDANCE

SEVENTEEN

HENRY BELLAKOFF

"Henry ! Henry, you're going to be late for work. Get your lazy self out of bed and get dressed, right now !"

"Okay, Mom, okay. I'm sorry. I'll be ready in a couple of minutes."

Whenever his mother yelled at him like that he thought about that old radio show tape Aunt Esther once played for him of a show called "The Aldrich Family" where every episode began with a woman's voice yelling "Henry...Henry Aldrich!" and the kid's response, in a teenager's cracked voice being, "Coming, Mother."

Henry was what almost anyone would call a good boy...a very good boy. His mother, however, tended to be extra strict with him because he reminded her so much of that wretched bastard who suddenly died and left her alone to care for herself and her two sons. According to her, he was never doing enough, and needed to be chastised and pushed.

Henry, now fourteen, remembered that before his father died suddenly, his mother was often the same way with her husband, even before she had a chance to resent him for "leaving" her. His father was a very nice person and a kind man who, while having considerable strength, would never willingly use it to hurt another man, woman, or child. Henry could see that his father really loved his mother, but she would frequently rebuff his loving or romantic offerings. Henry could also see sadness in his dad's reactions, and he and Barney used to wonder if he, with his striking good looks, ever had a girlfriend stashed away somewhere. He took the truthful answer to that question to his grave, and for Henry and Barney it remained a life-long mystery.

As for Barney, a really sweet kid, he could basically do no wrong in his mother's eyes, to the point that Barney would get embarrassed and apologize to his big brother. Barney felt blessed to have such a loving and protective older brother, and he learned on multiple occasions, that Henry, who hated fighting and violence and wouldn't, as they say, hurt a flea, could absolutely beat the crap out of anyone who posed a danger to his little brother. Henry had the "good kid but don't get him mad" reputation in the community, and Henry always avoided trouble whenever he could, even if he was sometimes called "chicken."

One of the kids he pounded the crap out of, as a proud Barney would declare, actually became a good friend of Henry's and was the person responsible for first getting Henry to the Boston Boxing Club. From his first visit, Henry was smitten with the Club and with boxing itself. The controlled use of physical power, the protective helmets, and padded gloves all spoke to the wish that boxing be a skilled combat sport, and not a wish to injure and destroy. Less than one year later he was to meet Bubba Dixon, and the rest, as they say, is history.

Henry's success in the ring, both as a teen age amateur and then as a pro was substantial, but always ahead of his success level outside the ring. His love of and growing devotion to boxing overshadowed a series of part-time jobs, where bosses wanted more time from him. His other failures involved a series of romantic relationships and break-ups with very attractive high school classmates. He never had trouble attracting women, or knowing how to please them, but he would eventually drive them away by becoming what they would call,"getting too serious too quickly". This was to remain a dynamic in Henry's adult love life also, a dynamic he was to never fully understand.

EIGHTEEN

NEW MEXICO AND ARIZONA REFLECTIONS

As Hank sped along the wide open, almost traffic free highways of New Mexico and Arizona, he took in the splendor of what was know as "Big Sky" type country where high rise building skylines and industrial air weren't clogging up one's senses.

He was smiling, feeling really free for the first time in his life...no people-obligations, no ugly streets and buildings, commercial and recreational places like stores and theaters absent and better yet, unimportant. Periodically, he would break into a little "La Bomba," and was now adding what he could remember of two old songs his father had played for him on his boxed record player: "Don't Fence Me In" and "Tumbling Tumbleweed."

His father had loved American cowboy movies and music, so Hank was more familiar with Gene Autry and Roy Rogers than a lot of other young boys his age, who were only into the Beatles and Elvis. His eyes misted over as he realized he had been thinking about his father more than usual lately, without being sure why.

There were also those moments when he thought about Donna, but surprisingly getting a cold chill type of feeling when he did. He thought to himself what a quick shift that was. By contrast, when he thought about Terry, he felt a warm flow of loving feelings, and some strong sexual ones, too. He would end those reflections with some sadness, and worry that he may have made a mistake not staying in West Texas. How often does a man encounter a woman who has so much to give him?

Hank had always felt so grateful when a woman would be very giving to him, but also a little uneasy with it because he never truly felt worthy of it. It was that gratefulness that would get him to jump in and fall in love so quickly. On the other hand, there were of course, women who reversed that process. Because of what some considered his good looks, Terry maybe being the most extreme example, and because of the really good body he had built up through lots of hours of hard training at the Club under Bubba's tutelage, there were some women who glommed on to him and quickly fell madly in love with him, and then raged at him when he told them in honesty that he did not feel the same way.

If given a choice, he of course preferred the incredible situation he wandered into with Terry to that other way, and he continued to have warm, hot, sad, and conflicted feelings about her. Terry certainly was great for his self esteem, and Susie would also have been if he had found her more.desirable. Hank was not a big male ego kind of guy ("egotesticle" he called them, and women with big egos he called "egotitsicle"). He always saw women as fully equal to men, and a few, like Bev, as superior to men. To him, communication was always key in relationships, and he was able to acknowledge that his own insecurities about worthiness sometimes messed that up. It would always take a lot for him to fall out of love, but again he noted how quickly he was doing that with Donna.

At times he would pass scenic areas that just about took his breath away, like canyons, pastel colored mountains, and then finally, the Hoover Dam, an awesome example of man's ingenuity. Eventually he entered California, with some desert driving, then Barstow, some precarious coastal mountain driving that was scary but also exciting, and then San Diego, what he hoped would become his new home.

As he drove around the city a little, he was struck by how clean it was, how wide the streets were, and the relatively placid feel to the place. Probably, he thought, it seemed that way only because of the part of the city he happened to be driving in.

He did see a lot of those seafood and Tex-Mex restaurants he had heard about, and also saw lots of Navy guys and a scattering of peep shows, strip clubs, and tattoo parlors near the waterfront. The temperature was as advertised, mild, and with a cool breeze. This definitely could be his new home, he thought.

He once again found a cheap hotel on the outskirts of the city, had a late night fish and chips dinner (Boston has better, he concluded), and slept like a log for ten hours. In the morning, he walked over to a small diner for breakfast, and sat there sipping coffee and pouring over the newspaper's classifieds on apartment rentals and job openings. He was definitely proceeding as though San Diego was indeed his new home.

NINETEEN
FEELING ADRIFT, AND THEN, KARYN

Hank's process for assimilating into and getting lost in the San Diego community went fairly quickly and smoothly. He took on the alias of Hank Westcott (Why that? He had no idea!) and avoided jobs that required both valid I.D. and Social Security number, i.e.,he worked on temporary jobs where he got paid "under the table," an odd and sometimes questionable approach to employment, but it was all he could do. He was traveling with a large amount of cash, his life savings, so to speak, obtained from cashing in his savings in a New Haven bank in between eating steamed hot dogs. He hoped to have no paper trail beyond New England, and he paid in cash for everything.

In contrast to his deplorable work situation, he found a lovely place to live, a well kept motel ("The Happy Gull") with rent by the month, a good size swimming pool, and excellent housekeeping service. Through his kitchen window he could see a piece of bright blue ocean, several large vessels, and bunches of tourists running to get to their next attraction.

The motel was owned by Marge Barlow, a very warm and friendly 55 year old widow, whose husband and co-owner Steve died suddenly three years ago, from a stroke. Marge was a bright capable woman who was carrying on with business quite well, but who would sometimes cry herself to sleep because of missing Steve quite a lot.

People seemed to keep to themselves pretty much, which Hank liked. He just felt safer here than all the other places he had been in since fleeing Boston. Marge managed the place wonderfully, with cleanliness and friendly customer service being things she stressed regularly with her staff. Her small attached coffee shop was actually much better than the nearby diner for breakfast, and Hank ate there every morning, except when he had to report very early for a job. Marge's pastries and coffee were really good, and her breakfast sandwiches awesome. Marge herself was an excellent conversationalist, and they soon became good friends. To some extent she was a partial replacement for Bubba, and for the female perspective, a substitute for Donna.The romantic, sexual Hank was in moth balls, memories of Terry being as close as he got to that.

However, that all changed in an instant, as such things have been known to do. It can also happen when you least expect it, and in this instance, Hank was sipping some of Marge's strong coffee in the Happy Gull Coffee Shop, not exactly the hub of anyone's universe, and it was an ungodly 7:05 a.m. on a rare rainy San Diego morning. Hank was the only customer when a pretty woman in a shiny royal blue raincoat and a young boy in a yellow rain outfit came in, a little out of breath. The woman collapsed their black umbrella and helped the boy out of his rain jacket. She then removed her coat and the two sat at one of the three small tables in the shop.

Hank, who was sitting at the four seat counter, swiveled to face the pair and said "Pretty wet out there, isn't it!" This was clearly one of the worst pick-up lines, if that's what it was meant to be, in Hank's entire life, including when he tried to hit on Lorraine Gillespie in the third grade.

"It is." was all the boy's mother, which Hank assumed she was, offered back.

Marge extended the thrilling conversation by adding, "What can I get you guys?"

The mother and son, looking at the one-card menu, exchanged a few mumblings, and then the mother said, "David's going to have a chocolate milk and a raspberry jelly doughnut, if you have that, and I'm going to have a coffee with just a little cream, and a cinnamon doughnut.

"Pleased to meet you, David," Marge responded, "and I do indeed have one raspberry jelly left, and now it's yours. So okay, he's David, I'm Marge, he's Hank, and you are___?"

Hank wondered if Marge had been reading his mind when she asked for the woman's name, something he was just itching to do himself, but feeling a bit too awkward to just do it. Well, awkward... maybe some...but it was more his fear that it could possibly be received as him trying to hit on her, which, of course, it really was.

"Hello, Marge...Hank...I`m Karyn, with a 'y' not an 'e'."

Hank and Marge, in almost perfect unrehearsed unison, replied, "Hello, Karyn," making the encounter sound like an AA meeting.

"You folks from around here?" Marge asked.

"No, we're from L.A. We're just down here on vacation. His dad and I had promised David we would take him to Mexico when he turned ten, and he did that last week, so here we are."

"So what's your husband doing, sleeping in?", Marge queried.

"Well actually no. He died last year in a car accident."

"Oh gosh, honey, I'm so sorry."

"That's okay," Karyn responded to Marge, but Hank could see both she and David held on to much sadness about the accident.

No one spoke for the next few minutes, Hank still sipping his coffee, and Karyn and David eating their breakfast treats. Hank found himself watching Karyn as much as he could without being obvious. She was a very beautiful woman in that no make-up natural way that Hank always loved, but never really had in the women he had relationships with. She was fair skinned, blue-eyed, appeared to be a natural blond, and had a definite Nordic look.

But what really captured Hank's attention the most was not her physical beauty, which did also include an appealing slim figure, but rather, the ways he saw Karyn responding to David. She would touch him in nurturing ways very frequently, and had a warm, attentive verbal style with him, both of which Hank loved watching. He found himself experiencing a flood of varied feelings about Karyn, all of which poured into his slightly overused "love at first sight" vessel, and left him feeling so attracted to her he could barely stand it.

At one point he and Marge exchanged that eyebrows raised smiling look that conveyed they were both quite taken with her. Marge could tell how much Hank was restraining himself from trying to make a move on this delightful creature, and she decided she needed to help him out.

"Have you ever been to Tijuana or other parts of Baja?"

"No, I haven't," Karyn responded, "We only moved down here from Minnesota two years ago, and a trip to Mexico was definitely on our list of things to do, but we just never got around to it."

Karyn's face flashed a look of grief for a moment, as she must have briefly reflected or her husband's untimely death, and then smiled at David and gently rubbed his shoulder.

"Well, you better be careful down there, especially in Tijuana," Marge advised. "It's still a bit of a shady place, if you catch my drift."

"Well, my plan is actually to go down to Ensenada. I think there'd be a lot there that David would love."

"Great plan, " Marge responded, and then, "Hey! Wait a minute! Hank, didn't you tell me you were planning to go down to Ensenada sometime this week?" As she said that, Marge turned fully toward Hank, once again smilingly making her eyebrows dance in a way that sent a very clear message that he should say yes.

"Actually I did say that," Hank lied. "I am."

TWENTY

THE TRIP

"Hey, David, are you ready for today's self defense lesson?"
"You bet, Hank. I'm totally ready."

This exchange between David Thorsen and Hank Westcott (his new name was becoming more comfortable every day) was rather amazing given that only two days had passed since "Marge's Breakfast and Dating Services" had created a connection between Hank and Karyn. When Hank moved over to their table to talk about Ensenada, the powerful attraction between Hank and Karyn, and the immediate ease and warmth between Hank and David, were right out there for all to see. In this case the "all" was Marge, who was just beaming with "I knew it!" type delight, watching it all unfold.

That same afternoon mother and son spent the day and early evening having fun with Hank in his Happy Gull home away from home, and when he offered to take them out for dinner, Karyn, uncharacteristically (she had been raised a strict Lutheran) simply said, "Okay. Thank you, Hank."

They had a very enjoyable dinner at a very kid-friendly burger joint, and then wished each other a good night. Hank clarified that he thought it would be best go to Ensenada three days later, and spend the next two days together getting to know each other better before their trip. Again Karyn, totally smitten with Hank, was very amenable to that plan.

The two had talked over the mechanics of the trip, i.e.she would pay for herself and David, and Hank would pay for himself, two separate rooms, the only displaying of their "obvious chemistry" (her term, much to Hank's delight) would be light, friendly hello and goodbye hugs if they so chose, and she would do the driving in her car and he would split the gas with her. She told Hank that since her husband Daniel's accident, neither she nor David had been driven by someone else, and she still needed

it to be that way. Hank was actually glad he wouldn't have to use his Bellakoff driver's license, and would probably be okay with his passport being his only potentially dangerous form of I.D.

The time spent over those next few days was almost magical for both, but none of that, of course, was put into words, just a lot of laughing and giggling, and many exchanges of glances with unmistakable meanings. Best of all was that David was part of it all, taking to Hank in a way that had once been reserved for his dad. Karyn was very tuned in to that relationship, and seeing it unfolding played an important role in her rapidly developing love feelings for this wonderful, good man on whom both she and David could rely.

Hank's feelings for Karyn were about as intense as any he could remember since his early days with Bev, but in some important way they were even better than back then. As he lay in bed trying to go to sleep the night before their trip, he was running a visual review through his mind of this whirlwind romance he was in when he got in touch with what it was that was different.

Even though he considered Karyn pretty damn close to Bev in the beauty department, he was spending much less time ogling her than he did Bev, and was actually more focused on watching this angelic woman nurture her son in such loving, beautiful ways.

His images of Karyn and David were suddenly jarred by a crystal clear image of his mother, poking him with an index finger whenever she was chastising him for his "laziness." Hank was almost awestruck by this rather obvious insight into his love and romance psyche, a path to better understanding himself that he had never taken before. He lay awake for several hours following parallels between his anguish and longings as a result of his mother's abusiveness, and his often overdriven and sometimes poorly chosen attempts to find love and nurturance from a woman. By the time he started to fall asleep, Hank was feeling as though he had just grown as a person in some important way.

———

By the time he first laid eyes on Karyn the next morning in the coffee shop, Hank was feeling more deeply in love than ever. Whether that was a manifestation of personal growth or not wasn't really on his mind as he devoured one of Marge's great breakfast sandwiches, drank his coffee, and delighted in seeing Karyn looking very happy and, like David, excited about their trip.They both joined in on the breakfast sandwich idea, and soon the three were ready to take off.

After Hank placed his bag next to theirs in the trunk of Karyn's car, a light blue Volvo wagon (supposedly extra resistant to collision damage), he returned to the coffee shop to join in saying to Marge that they would send her a postcard. Marge told them to slow down a minute, because there was something she wanted to say.

"Look, you guys, do you realize how great you three look together? I knew from the minute you walked into the shop that something out of the ordinary was going to happen, and it sure did. I love you guys, and I want to take your picture before you go. I'll give you a copy when you get back."

After Marge took their picture, the three hopped into the Volvo and took off for their Mexican adventure, an adventure that would prove to be more than they bargained for.

TWENTY-ONE

ENSENADA

The trip from the Happy Gull to the border was very short and uneventful. The crossing itself took several hours, with most of that time spent waiting in a long line of cars. They were sure the border patrol agent assumed they were a married couple because he seemed a little surprised as he looked at Hank's passport which would, of course, in Karyn's mind, contain the name Westcott. Hank hoped she herself wouldn't look at the passport as she passed it back to him, because if she saw the name Bellakoff, there would be lot of explaining to do that might put a damper on this potentially idyllic trip.

She didn't.

However, the whole issue of his identity stirred up enough anxiety in Hank that as soon as he could find a pay phone in Tijuana, he got out and called Susie, this being his first opportunity to call without using a traceable California phone number.

His conversation with her was fairly brief, much to her disappointment. Susie was still hoping Hank would sooner or later give in to her feminine wiles. He asked her to tell him if anything noteworthy in the world of crime was going on in Boston, and whether he was still being written about in the local sports pages. She said no to both, and assured Hank she read the entire Boston Globe every day.

They concluded with her asking him if he was coming back to Boston soon, where was he staying now, and would he promise to come and see her when back in town. He told her he would not be back for quite a while, that he would come see her when he did, that he needed this phone call to be a secret, and that he was living in New Haven. The last piece of misinformation was a gift to her in case mob guys started checking neighbors. If she had some information she believed was the truth, under extreme pressure she might cough it up, and they would accept that she was telling all she knew, especially if they uncovered his dead end paper trail in New Haven. In short, it was misinformation that might help keep her alive if Tweedledum and Tweedledee ever tried to work her over.

All three of the happy travelers agreed Tijuana was a rather grungy, unappealing place, with hordes of bargain-seeking tourists filling the incredibly dusty downtown streets. They followed Mexico Route 5 to Ensenada, but spent almost four hours doing it. Between occasional stops for scenery, several bathroom breaks, and a leisurely lunch in scenic, but also somewhat grungy Rosarito Beach, it was mid-afternoon before they reached their destination.

Ensenada, compared to anything else they had seen in Baja California, was a shining jewel of a small oceanside town, with tourists, of course, but people who seemed relaxed and to appreciate that the real bargain here was Ensenada itself.

After getting their two rooms in a hotel recommended in Karyn`s tour book, they sat outside on their oceanfront patio watching the gigantic Pacific waves come crashing in towards them, but a safe distance away. David said he was feeling ocean spray, and while Hank and Karyn weren't, they didn't disagree, not wanting to put a damper on the excited boy's feeling damp.

It was too cool for them to use the motel swimming pool, and it looked like a rainstorm could be coming soon, so the three took off for downtown Ensenada, planning to do some shopping and sight-seeing.

Throughout the day many pictures were taken, but almost all by Hank. Most were of Karyn and David with scenic backdrops, ranging from a huge wave to a great photo with an old taco street vendor, with his products produced on a small grill set inside a large metal wheelbarrow. Mounds of cut up peppers and onions and cheeses surrounded the grill, and there were several types of whole hot peppers. Between the food and the old man's serape, the colors were stunning. Hank avoided being in any photos until Karyn insisted she take one of him with David in front of a Jai Alai stadium, and David insisted on taking one of his mother and Hank in front of a horse and carriage used for tourists.

As a light rain started they ran into a small bistro type restaurant for a genuine Mexican meal, and then sat at one of the outdoor tables of the Rooster Bar next door, doing some people watching, and playing several word games as they sipped minted iced tea. By the end of the day the exhausted trio headed back to their hotel. With the weather still not good for pool swimming, they all agreed to take a nap, and the get together to plan dinner. Hank seized on the opportunity to give Karyn a "see ya' later" hug, and she accepted it just enough for his head to start swirling with images and sensations of what it would be like to make love to this woman. As beautiful as that all was, Hank couldn't avoid a few moments of recollections of having sex with Terry, but he concluded there was nothing wrong with that.

———

It was now dark outside, very breezy, and a full four hours after they parted for naps. They all agreed they were more tired than they realized. Now they were extremely hungry, but discovered when they went back to the center of town, that Ensenada was not the same as Tijuana, which was famous for late or all night places for eating, partying, gambling, whatever you were looking for. Some places were already closed, the tourists in the streets mostly gone, as well as the street vendors.

There were a fair number of restaurants that provided fine dining, a few that were probably cheaper but unsafe, and to David's delight, a Kentucky Fried Chicken place that seemed to be one of the busiest places in town. Karyn asked Hank if he was okay with that choice, and he responded truthfully by revealing his life-long addiction to their food. After David told him he was the coolest guy he ever met, they entered and devoured a Family Bucket, along with some refried beans and rice in place of the ubiquitous mashed potato and gravy.

"When in Rome, eat what the Romans eat", Hank quipped. Even David understood that one. After dinner, they strolled out onto the street, and were about to head to the car when Hank got a powerful urge to pee.

"Do you guys mind going back in for just a couple of minutes?"

Karyn replied that because the rain had stopped and the air felt so fresh and cool, they would rather wait outside for him. Hank accepted that and quickly headed back into the KFC to do his business. Several men were in the bathroom when he got there, and he had to wait a few minutes, then did his thing and left.

When he got back out onto the street he saw that Karyn and David were directly across the wide avenue, surrounded by four young Mexican guys, with one of them right up close to her and obviously harassing her.

"Hi, Hank," Karyn called out, as she could see him from the corner of her eye; at least she hoped it was Hank. Her voice had a clear sense of urgency in it, bordering on desperation.

"Coming, honey. And hey, you boys go home now," he called out as he raced across the street. When he got up close he could see how terrified Karyn must be, because while two of the men looked like ordinary kids, barely out of their teens, the other two, especially the one breathing on Karyn, and also the one blocking the space between her and David, looked older, meaner, and more threatening.

"Hey, you old *gringo*, why don't YOU go home?" All four men laughed, but Hank was in no laughing mood.

"Look you guys, I am not looking for any trouble, so I'm simply going to ask you to back off right now and leave us alone, okay?"

"And if we don't want to?" asked the breather.

"Listen, don't make that mistake. Just back off and leave. NOW!"

The breather turned toward Hank, took one step forward, and said "No way. Your lady, she's too hot for me to leave." He then made that disgusting lip-sucking cat calling sound that too many men in the world made lewdly in reference to women.

"Big mistake", Hank said softly as he took his own forward step so that now the breather was breathing on him. He knew his strategy in dealing with the four would simply be to destroy the first guy badly enough to scare off the others, something he knew he could easily do. He was just a little reluctant because he didn't like using his fists to destroy people (his mind flashed to a prone, bleeding Archie for a brief moment), but the gross disrespect for Karyn was enough to resolve the conflict for Hank.

Hank blocked his opponents first swing with his left arm, and then planted his right fist into the guy's gut, causing the man to let out a yelp as he doubled over in pain, and then, feeling no mercy, delivered a powerful left uppercut to the guy's totally exposed chin, not unlike the punch he had used to nail Archie. No yelp was emitted this time, and the man was unconscious before he landed on his back with a thud a few feet away.

"You guys have one minute to get him and yourselves out of here, or I will seriously hurt every one of you."

With no delay, the three started dragging their friend away. When they were a safe distance from Hank, the one who had been blocking David from his mother, called out to Hank through gritted teeth, with hatred in his eyes, "We'll remember you, *gringo*, and if we meet again in Ensenada, you are a dead man."

Hank had no doubt of the man's sincerity, but turned his attention to Karyn and engaged in a prolonged intense hug emanating not from passion, but from relief, and manifesting the loving gratefulness they each felt for the other. David grabbed onto both of them, absorbing and sharing those identical feelings.

The three then got quickly to Karyn's car and headed back to the hotel. Hank offered to sleep on some blankets on the floor in their room, and Karyn was still too shaken to refuse.

"Yippee", said David, and a kind of yippee Hank also thought to himself.

TWENTY-TWO

AT THE HAPPY GULL

Hank lay on the floor, about six or seven feet from Karyn's side of the bed, facing her. He had the help of four thin blankets and two pillows heavily stuffed with duck feathers, which, while not at all as comfortable as luxurious goose down, was not bad at all. The blankets, however were quite thin and the floor hard, and they made him yearn for the comforters and heavy blankets usually found in New England motels.

But cold he wasn't. As he watched Karyn drift off, he felt that warm glow he always felt when near her. The last thing he remembered about falling asleep, was a moment when they were both looking straight at each other, the heat palpable, and both wearing slight smiles. He sluggishly kissed the fingertips of his left hand and wiggled them in her direction, all of it like a semi-narcoleptic blowing a goodnight kiss.

However, he awoke with a start less than an hour later, finding himself almost overwhelmed by his senses being flooded, because snuggled up beside him on the floor was Karyn. He smelled an insanely floral scent. Her hair, in which his hand was now entangled, felt like pure silk, her right hand which was cupping the left side of his head generated great warmth as she gently stroked his ear with her thumb, and her breath was oh so warm as she lowered her full lips onto his. It lasted for a few blissful moments, the kiss of his lifetime.He made small murmuring sounds, as did she, and she whispered, "Shhh...we don't want to wake up David." Hank nodded, and they just hugged silently, tightly, making the most beautiful type of non-genital love.

It became apparent that even though Karyn had planned to crawl back into her bed, she never got there. In what seemed like only a few minutes, she and Hank had fallen asleep together and now, with sunlight pouring into their room through the cheap curtains, David was sitting on the edge of the bed telling them to wake up so they can all get breakfast.

"Mom," he said, "I want you to know I think it's very cool, you and Hank being together like that, okay?"

"Okay ", Karen blushingly responded, with Hank adding, "I knew I liked you, kid.", smiling, but also flashing once again to his lost pal, Bubba.

They quickly got dressed and headed out to a small nearby restaurant, with the terrifying events of the night before just now starting to creep back in.

"Are we all agreed we head north after breakfast?", asked Karyn. The two men in her life agreed.

When David later excused himself to go to the bathroom, Hank grabbed Karyn's hand, face strained with the need to verbalize his feelings, and sputtered, "Oh God, Karyn,...I want..."

"Shhh", Karyn responded, shushing him for the second time in just a few hours. "Hank, I know. I feel it too...We've become a family, haven't we...In just a matter of days...and it feels so real."

David returned to the two of them doing that hugging-holding thing they did, and jokingly teased the two of them, with, "Hey you two, let's not overdo it. What will people think?"

When they got back to their rooms, they packed very quickly, paid their final bill, and sped out to Route 5 North, leaving behind the little romantic sparkling jewel of a town, where magical things happened, and where Hank had been promised an early death.

They stopped for a few hours in Tijuana, long enough for David to buy a souvenir he really wanted, a *sombrero* with thin multi-colored cloth bands, round the top and just over and around the rim. They also drank more minted iced tea at the Rooster, and ate more tacos from the same street vendor. But, as they were leaving, they all agreed that the "Big T" was not their cup of tea, and adding that to the deadly consequences of ever returning to Ensenada, it was, as David said (a few too many annoying times on the trip back to San Diego), "Bah, Bah, Baja!" David was a great kid, but even great kids can annoy.

The Border lines were longer than on the way in, with many cars being searched for drugs and other contraband. At one point, while being searched, Karyn said to an agent, "Look, all we want to bring back to the States is a ten year old boy and his hat for bed time. And we'll even surrender his *sombrero* if we have to."

"You'll just have to be patient; this is not a game, Mrs. Bellakoff."

"Mrs. *who?* My god, you don't even know my identity after all this time?"

Hank loved Karyn's feistiness, but this was one time he wished she would have kept quiet.

"Hey, Honey, let's relax and we'll talk about it later."

Karyn wheeled around to look Hank in the eye and said, "Hank, what is this, what's going on?"

"Karyn, let's go sit over there and talk."

Karyn, summoning up the trust she still had in this wonderful man, agreed to stop, and three headed for the long wooden bench in the waiting room.

"Who is Bellakoff?"

"I am."

"Then who is Hank Westcott?"

"That is my new name."

"Why do you have a fake new name?" At this point, they had David attempting to follow it all, but him not being sure he could.

"When I moved here a while back I needed to leave behind my real identity."

"Why?" Karyn was visibly quite upset, and was not mincing her words.

"Because I was in danger back home and needed for some very bad people to never find me."

"In Rhode Island?"

Here Hank paused, and needed to quickly decide if he could go all the way with Karyn and trust, and in fact, with Karyn in life. He found it a quick and easy decision.

"No, Massachusetts...Boston."

"What? You lied about where you came from? Hank, I love you... What did you do in Boston?"

"Karyn, there's a long story here we need to save for later, over dinner in San Diego. Just believe me when I tell you I have never in my life committed any crime, none whatsoever...please."

Karyn took a deep breath for the first time since she was called Mrs. Bellakoff, and sat back on the uncomfortable bench.

"Are the bad people still looking for you? Are they in California?" David was picking up for his mother, asking very practical ten-year-old boy questions, primarily about were he and his mother in danger too.

"David, as far as I know, they may look for me forever, but, no. No one is here, and no one knows I'm here." That last part was something he wanted the boy to believe, even though he couldn't be sure about it himself.

"Karyn, please, can we wait for later? I promise I'll explain everything to you." He looked at Karyn as he said that, and could see her struggling with his words.

"Goddamnit, Karyn, David knows this better than you do. I am so in love with you, and I want a life with you, so PLEASE, just trust me until dinner, and let this all go for now."

David added, "Mom, he's right. I know you know he loves you, and that he really wants us to be a family, so can't you just wait?"

With David's words, Karyn's countenance changed dramatically, with one of her magical moist-eyed smiles emerging, and within a moment, all three were once again hugging.

Soon they were on the road north to San Diego, obviously no one in a Mexican jail for trying to smuggle *sombreros*, and all three itching to get back. As they approached San Diego, Hank suggested to his companions that they dine at Long John Silver's. Since Karyn and his dad were never fast food types, Hank had to explain to David that L.J.S. was a lot like K.F.C., except inside that unhealthy, crunchy, deliriously delicious coating was fish instead of chicken. David, who did like fish, agreed.

Hank chose a table in a back corner of the dining area, somewhat separate from tables with people at them. As they ate their meal, Hank started what was to be a lengthy soliloquy about his pre-San Diego life, trying his best to censor certain things for David, but also hoping not to reveal anything that could endanger them down the road.

He talked a little about his childhood, no dad after age 12 and a very strict mother who favored his younger brother, about high school, and jobs, and meeting Bubba, and the Club, and his career up to the fight with Archie, and Bubba's gambling issues, and what the mob did to Bubba and would now do to him if they ever found him. He referred to Bev and Donna as his two significant involvements over the years, and left it at that.

"So last night, when you beat up that creep, you were in your element,"observed Karyn. Her choice of the word "element" bothered Hank, because it made it sound like he hung out in a trashy world. He expressed that feeling to her, and she immediately apologized, saying she really meant that for him, being in the fight was a natural and comfortable situation.

"I did note what a powerful man you are, and ferocious."

"Yeah, Hank, you were awesome," added David.

"I was scared also, afraid that if I didn't succeed, something bad would happen to you guys. But listen, David, you've got to promise me you're not going to talk about the fight with anyone,...at school, or anywhere."

"Why?"

"Why? Because in this country a professional fighter can be accused of murder or attempted murder very easily when there's a fight, because his fists are considered lethal weapons, just like if he used a gun or a knife."

"Will that guy from last night accuse you of attempted murder?"

"I doubt it, David, because it happened in Mexico, and i think the laws are different there."

"Whew! I'm glad of that, Hank."

"And what about you?", Hank asked, turning toward Karyn. He was trying hard to read her expression, but he couldn't.

"Oh God, Hank. There's so much for me to digest with all this, and right now I'm exhausted and need to get some sleep."

"Okay, Karyn. Can we meet in the morning for breakfast at Marge's?" Karyn could see how fearful Hank was of possible rejection from her, and with their heading back up to L.A. after breakfast, she needed to send him a quick and clear message.

"I want a life with you, Hank, and that won't change, but we need to be able to smooth out the bumps in the road as we go on our journey together. Just be patient with me..."

She embraced Hank, and then gave him a very unequivocal lingering kiss, even though David was obviously watching. Hank's eyes filled with tears, and he held on to her tightly for a minute, and then said with a smile, "Okay, cowboys and girls, let's hit the road!"

When they got to the Happy Gull, Hank hopped out of the car, grabbed his bag out of the trunk, blew them both a kiss, and called out, "See you in the morning!" as they drove off. Hank's heart sank a little as he watched the car turn the corner and disappear. "She's my future," he thought to himself, and "I will love her for the rest of my life."

———

Hank headed for the front office to tell Marge all the news, or at least most of it. She wasn't there behind the desk reading a book and drinking tea as she usually was, so he headed for his room, figuring he'd catch up with her later.

Hank unlocked the door of his home away from home, and as he entered and closed the door behind him, he had a brief flashback to when he entered his apartment and saw the warning written on his bathroom mirror. Be a good boy? He WAS a good boy, is a good boy, and maybe never was as bad a boy as he should have been. He knew he was too much of a pleaser, but didn't know how to be any other way. He was realizing how much fear and stress he was experiencing today, working so hard to avoid displeasing Karyn. He started to remember the dream ...the one he had repeatedly all through high school.

He is in his elementary school building, on the upper floor that has a very long corridor that ends at the big stairway used to get to the lower floor. The building is not lighted, but the moon is giving it just enough light to be able to see. The building seems empty but as he stands at one end of the corridor, Henry suddenly sees a light coming out of a room way down on the right, very close to the distant stairway. Henry sees that it is his mother coming out of that room and he calls out to her, telling her it's him, Henry, and she should wait for him to go down the corridor to join her. His mother pauses, sees that it is him, and turns toward the stairway. He calls out several times pleading with her to wait for him as he races through the hallway toward where she is. But, she doesn't wait, and starts going down the stairs. Henry is now running toward the stairs, but his mother continues down the stairs to the point that he can no longer see her. When he gets to the stairs he doesn't stop running, and after catching the top stair with one foot, he is hurtling through the air, open space, no stairs, and he's falling...and falling...

At that point, he always woke up, with cold sweats and shaking for a few moments, and then back to sleep. He remembered hearing from a classmate that if you don't land in a falling dream, that's a good thing, because if you do land, then it's a death dream. So he would use that thought to shake any lingering bad feelings from thew dream.

Hank sat in his recliner and relaxed for a few minutes, trying to let the emotional stressors of the entire time since meeting Karyn pass through and then out of his body.

He got up to get a cold beer out of the refrigerator, wishing it was the Sham instead, drank some in his recliner, and then nodded off for a few minutes.

He awoke abruptly to the sound of a voice saying, "Hello, Hank." A male voice. As his eyes slowly opened two male figures came into his focus. One, about ten feet away, was a slender, youngish-looking mustached guy wearing jeans and a plain black t-shirt. He was probably in his early twenties, but more importantly, held a long barreled gun pointed squarely at him.

The other man was older, maybe late thirties, wearing jeans and a black sleeveless t-shirt with a large white skull and crossbones emblazoned on the front. He was only a few feet away, standing right in front of Hank with arms folded, and trim bearded face smiling at him. He was big,...really big. While it was hard for Hank to estimate his size with the man so close to him, and his eyes still a little sticky, and struggling to adapt to the light in the room, Hank guessed that he had to be at least six-three, very heavily muscled, almost alarmingly so, and probably around two-twenty or thirty. As a boxer, Hank had to be quite good at estimating men's weight. This guy looked like he probably lifted weights.

"Hello," Hank responded, not one of his more macho responses to danger. His mind was rapidly trying to assess who these two were, but while Boston mob would have been a very logical guess, the t-shirts and jeans did not match up, and left him perplexed.

"Who are you?", he asked, as he was beginning to be more fully awake...and scared.

"I'm Jack Slocum."

"Is that supposed to men something to me?"

"It should, smart-ass." Slocum moved two menacing steps closer, and Hank could now see the brass knuckles and several large rings this Goliath had on each hand...

"What do you want with me? Are you from Beantown?" Hank asked, afraid of the likely answer.

"Where the fuck is Beantown?"

Hank's heart stopped pounding so fiercely, and he was now no longer thinking this could be his final minutes alive. No matter who Slocum was, Hank had a fighting chance,...literally.

"So what's your beef with me and why is Gabby Hayes over there?"

"Watch your mouth, asshole. Billy is my friend, and he`s here to help keep things under control."

"Meaning ?"

"Meaning he plans to watch me beat the livin' shit out of you, and he will start shooting holes into your arms or legs if he sees you trying to stop me. You wanna look like Swiss cheese, just put up some fight."

"Why me? What did I do to you?"

"You didn't hear me say my name was Slocum?"

"I did, but is that supposed to tell me something?"

"Son-of-a-bitch, she didn't tell you her last name, did she?"

"Who didn't?"

"Listen, Hank lover boy, I'm Terry Slocum's husband."

"You're Terry's husband?"

"Is there a friggin' echo in this room ? Yeah, Terry is my wife, and you've been messin' around with my woman!"

"Oh jeez man, I didn't know she was married. She never said a word about it, and she had no ring. I don't mess with other men's women."

Donna flashed into his mind, but just for a second, not enough to stop him from doubling down on his lie about ethics. "I just don't believe in doing that."

"I'm still going to beat you bad, man." Jack Slocum was now declaring to do what Hank could not let him do, if he could help it. He stood up as Slocum came at him and then ducked under his big metal-enhanced fist. Hank planted two quick punches to the big guys kidney spot, with little effect. He was solid muscle. Jack swung again, and this time he caught Hank on the shoulder, just grazing it, but enough to take off some skin and bring on the blood.

Hank could see Billy in the background, pointing his gun straight at him, so he took a big side step as Jack lunged at him again. Jack was now between him and Billy, making a shot impossible for Billy. Hank landed a looping left hook smack in the middle of Jack Slocum's face, probably breaking his nose, and as Jack angrily cursed Hank and the pain, Hank made his move, lowering his head and charging straight into the bigger man's chest. Hank pistoned his legs, the ones Bubba called among the best he had ever seen on a boxer, as hard as he could. And like a great blocking football offensive lineman, he shoved the screaming Jack back into Billy, mashing him against the wall, his gun now on the floor.

Both Billy and Jack went down like two sacks of potatoes. Billy appeared unconscious, but Jack got up quickly on his own powerful legs, and charged Hank with his two menacing fists ready to do their damage to this wife-banging bastard. But Hank, ready for the attack, swung from his heels, as they say, and landed a vicious right uppercut to Jack's chin. It was as hard a punch as he had ever thrown in his life, and the excruciating pain from his untaped, ungloved fist told him he had likely broken it, along with Jack's jaw.

The force of that punch sent Jack reeling backwards into the oak bureau behind him, the one, unfortunately, with the sharp-edged corners. His head struck a corner and he slumped to the floor, looking lifeless. Within a minute Hank began to see the slowly developing blood pool oozing from his head. Hank, feeling scared and that Bill Russell nausea creeping in, knelt down and turned Jack Slocum's face toward him. The partially opened, but unmoving eyes conveyed clearly to Hank that he had just murdered Terry Slocum's secret husband. He then completed the puking process, and for a minute or two had trouble catching his breath.

Just as Hank was beginning to pay attention to his own bleeding shoulder, he heard a moaning sound from Billy who was beginning to stir.

TWENTY-THREE
RUNNING DOWNWARD

As Billy stirred, Hank was hit by a terrifying reality, that there was a surviving witness to his murder of Jack Slocum. Hank picked up the gun and pointed it at Billy as Jack Slocum's young protector slowly stood up, trying to clear his head. As he did so, he groaned a few times when he experienced pains from parts of his body that had gotten especially hard hit by his old buddy's massive torso. Each pain, however, also seemed to help clear his mind, so that when he was finally standing upright, his eyes immediately started darting around the room looking for Jack. When he finally spotted the motionless body on the rug with the small pool of blood, he simply uttered, "Oh, holy shit!"

"Alright, Billy Boy, so I'm not a killer, and what happened to Jack, who came here with you to mess me up, was an accident. He hit his head on the edge of the dresser after he fell into you".

"Bullshit, man, that dresser is over there, not here. You did something else to him."

"Yeah, Billy Boy, I punched him in the face as he lunged at me with those brass knuckles, and he fell into the dresser. You assholes never should have come here in the first place."

"Oh really, after you did his wife? What would you do! Well, he messed up that spic bitch waitress who told him what happened, and he got your picture from her or Terry, You weren't that hard to find when Terry told him you were headed here.

"What did Jack do to the two women?"

"Huh, oh nothing much to Terry, just one punch to her belly. He wouldn't want to mess up that face, and she's done shit a few times before, and she'd be dead or crippled by now if he ever did more than that to her."

"And the waitress?"

"Oh, he messed that bitch up real good." "Did he kill her?"

"Naw, just broke a few things."

"I should kill you, but I won't. I'm going to leave you here to meet the cops. But I'll shoot you in the head right now", Hank said through gritted teeth and touching the tip of the gun barrel to Billy's cheek, "unless you tell me where Marge is."

"Who?"

"Marge, the woman who owns this place. What did you scumbags do to her?"

"Jack messed her up a little because she didn't want him to find you. She's not dead, she's tied up and gagged in her bathroom."

"Come with me right now, so I can see for myself. If she's dead, Billy Boy, so are you."

They found Marge bound and gagged, but conscious. Hank ordered Billy to remove the tape, and Hank then applied the same tape to Billy, who was now bound and gagged himself, and would be there to meet the cops after Marge called 911.

Hank explained everything to Marge, who had swollen and cut lips, and many ugly bruises on her face and neck. He explained that he needed to run immediately, told her she was a great friend, and gave her a hug and a kiss on her forehead.

As he was just about out the door, Marge yelled out to Hank to stop for a minute, saying she needed to tell him something.

"The morning of your trip, Karyn called me to thank me for

bringing you into her life, and told me how amazing it was that I could tell right away that you and she would connect. She said 'Marge, I intend to make at least one baby with that man, and I`m telling you that just a few days after you played Cupid. I'll be grateful to you forever.' I wanted you to know that, Hank. That girl really loves you."

Hank just stood there for a moment, fighting back tears, absorbing what Marge had just told him, and asked Marge to tell Karyn he loved her that way too, and that he would call her if Marge would give him the phone number. Marge quickly scrawled Karyn`s home phone number in L.A., handed it to Hank, and sighed, as she watched this lovely man go out the door.

She then reached for her phone to call the police, and have them come to the Happy Gull.

———

Hank drove out of San Diego quickly, and definitely not singing "La Bomba." He was leaving his home away from home, probably permanently, and he struggled with the dreadful fear that he might never see Karyn and David again.

As he hit the outskirts of San Diego, he briefly thought of turning north to Los Angeles, but knowing that would only set him up for capture by police or a hit from Boston, he turned south to the Border. Hiding somewhere in the Baja Peninsula was his best hope for survival, as long as he by-passed Ensenada.

Hank stopped for a quick enchilada meal in Rosarito Beach, but spent several hours looking through a Guide to Baja California book, reading up on small towns south of Ensenada that might work out for him. He began to focus on Santo Rosalia, a small seaside town that used to be a copper mining town, but was now just a quiet, non-resort town of about 14,000 people with an active ferry boat system to the Mexican mainland. The escape to the mainland concept struck Hank as a nifty safety valve, so to speak, so he set his sights on the little town nine hours further south on Mexico Route 1.

He made only two stops before he reached Santo Rosalia, one for a gas and toilet break, and one for coffee and pastry to keep him awake. It was dark when he arrived in Santo Rosalia, and while he was interested in staying in one of the cliffside motels he had read about, he settled for a fairly rundown one just outside the small downtown area.

When he woke up in the morning in the very depressing surroundings that can only be provided by a fleabag motel, Hank did the unavoidable reflecting about what an incredible downward turn his life had taken since the fight with Archie. If only he could replay that fatal round and...and what? Would his life have been totally different if he had held back that fatal punch? Donna, Schumacher, Bubba, Terry, Karyn and David? Would anything be like it is now, with him in a shit box motel half-way down the Mexican Baja Peninsula, afraid to be out in the world, one alias already and now a need for a new one?

Hank knew only one thing for sure, he needed to get good and goddamned drunk, and maybe a cup of coffee, also.

He asked the young Mexican guy at the desk where he could buy a bottle, and the kid pointed to a small store with no sign across the dirt road. Hank used U.S. dollars to buy a bottle of cheap tequila; in Hank's mind they all tasted the same, like medicinal vomit. He also got a small styrofoam cup of stale hot coffee and an equally stale Yankee Doodle Devil Dog pastry, and brought all three treasures back to his squalid new "home away from home". God, how he was growing to hate that expression.

Hank heavily spiked his coffee with the rotgut Tequila Supremo so that his coffee now tasted like coffee flavored medicinal vomit, and eventually washed down the rest of his pastry brunch with straight rotgut. He thought he could feel a hole opening in his stomach as he drank it. The warm buzz he ended up with felt good, and he decided drinking might be his only way to get through this chapter in his life.

Hopefully, this was just a chapter. What would be his future chapters? How about "Hank returns permanently to the U.S.," "Hank moves to L.A.," " Hank marries Karyn, and David is co- Best Man with Bubba Dixon," "Hank and Karyn have Liam," and "Hank and Karyn become grandparents.".A few more swallows from the bottle and he thought, naw, just one more: "Renegade Boxer Found Dead in Mexico, and the newspapers declare there is a growing list of possible perpetrators."

Hank fell asleep but awoke to the desk kid knocking on his door, telling him he needed to pay more, or leave. Hank chose the latter, and decided to drive up to the cliffside motels while it was still light out. To his surprise, the majority of the motels were quite decent looking, and the Sea of Cortez, way down below, was a dazzling sight. Getting too close to cliff's edge at night would probably be a bad idea, although Hank noticed that a few of the motels had outdoor night lights.

He eventually chose the Cortez Grande Motel, because while it had no outside nightlight, it had the biggest sea-view picture windows. As he emptied his bag into the bureau and bathroom cabinet, he thought that here it is, his new home away from home, but that he, at this point, was essentially homeless. That called for two sizable swigs of rotgut tequila, replete with that delightful "stomach on fire, stomach on fire" after effect. An hour later he had emptied his bottle, emptied his bladder, and was stone cold asleep for the night, at least until 5:45 a.m. At that point he emptied his bladder again, tried to suck a few drops of tequila from the empty bottle, and fell asleep again until noon.

Hank had learned a little bit of Spanish vocabulary from the Latino fighters who came through the Club, and also when in Puerto Rico for a week when he fought and badly beat Hector Renato, an up and coming young fighter who was supposedly a threat to pass Hank in the Division rankings if he won the fight. It was an overwhelming unanimous decision for Hank, and little was heard from Renato after that, at least partly because Hank had humiliated him in front of his fellow Puerto Ricans. He sometimes wondered if he was being punished for that, and for Archie, and for cuckolding Jack Toohey, and....now for killing Jack Slocum ? "Oh Christ I need some tequila !"

Hank used a little of his limited Spanish to buy some tequila, this time a grade better than the last one, at the same store.This one was called Black Sombrero Tequila, a slightly ominous name, but it certainly went down the gut with a lot less fire. He thought that Tequila Supremo probably had a turpentine additive, and that Black Sombrero was now his drink of choice. Actually Hank, not that big a drinker, never had a drink of choice, the Schlitz beer at the Sham the closest to being one.

He also purchased some canned corned beef, a packaged devil dog, two small bottles of orange juice, a small bottle of hot sauce and a loaf of real, actual, genuine Wonder Bread, something he loved as a kid, but didn't think they even made anymore. He also bought a few medium sized cigars, probably Cuban, and spent the evening partying with and loving his unhealthy bounty.

———

Henry was wary of his mother discovering him at the refrigerator scooping some left over potato salad out of a bowl with his fingers, and chomping on a cold hot dog. He had gotten home late from work, and his mother had refused to make him the dinner she had made for Barney and herself, saying he was late, she was tired, and that he should do his homework and go to bed. While she really didn't mean that he should have no supper, just that she wasn't going to make it for him. Henry, however, took her literally, didn't want to do anything to displease her, and went to bed not having eaten. Now it was 3:00 a.m., he had to be up in two-and-a-half hours for his newspaper job, but he was too hungry to sleep. He finished with two packaged chocolate chip cookies, a little milk, and went to bed. Within twenty minutes he was soundly sleeping.

Henry's Dream

Within an hour he was lying on a blanket in the hot sun at Winthrop Beach, his dad's favorite. He was around six years old, overweight, shy, and a really, really good kid, quiet and well behaved. His favorite thing to do at the beach besides being in the water, was to play catch with his dad, using a small pink rubber ball. But his dad isn't there on this day. Henry is there with his Aunt Naomi and Cousin Janette, who offered to take him to the beach, because Barney, being a very pale-skinned red head, burns badly in the sun, and Henry's mother always wants to stay at home in the shade with poor Barney.

At one point in the very hot afternoon, Aunt Naomi says, "Come on, Henry, come down to stand in the cold water with Cousin Janette and me. I don't want to leave you alone here."

Henry agrees, and soon is standing waist deep in the cold refreshing ocean water, holding on to Aunt Naomi's hand while she and Janette are arguing about something. Henry gets the really great idea of doing a somersault under the water, something he had tried before because he saw a friend do it. He has probably tried it ten times before, but can never complete it because he gets too much water up his nose. He lets go of Aunt Naomi's hand, but she's too busy arguing with Janette to notice. He dips his head down into the cold salt water, then brings his arms around near his head as if he was diving, and then, pushing his feet off the sandy bottom, he plunges down into the cold and dark world below with his eyes closed. The flip starts to develop, but then, as with every try before, he bumps his head on the bottom, his nose fills up with stinging salty water, his arms start to flail, and he is immediately flat on his back on the bottom. Unlike other times, he panics, and can't seem to get up, and as he struggles, he envisions a stream of images from his brief six year old life, and figures he is doing what he has heard people do when they're dying. He gives a giant push with his feet, and within moments, is standing up again in waist deep water, shivering a little, and shaken to the core by his secret near death excursion. He take Aunt Naomi's hand again, and never tells anyone about it...ever.

He remembers his dad once telling him of a panic experience he once had as a teenager in which he was competing underwater with friends to see if they could swim the whole length of the pier they were on without coming up for air. Several friends had already done it, but when his dad tried to go the whole way he panicked, and afraid he was going to drown, he desperately stuck two fingers up between the slats of the pier. He was saved by a friend who saw what was happening, jumped off the side of the pier, and pulled his dad out from under. When his dad joins the three of them on the blanket later on, Henry doesn't tell him what happened. He just climbs into his dad's royal blue boxer bathing trunks-clad lap, and finally feels safe, as his dad encircles him with his arms and gives him an affectionate hug.

Henry is out the door in the morning before his mother and Barney wakes up, rushing to get his big stack of Boston Globe newspapers so he can start his deliveries.

———

Hank woke up at noon, famished. He was getting sick of dining on Devil Dogs, tacos, and canned meat, and hadn't had a real meal in days. He longed for a big plate of carne assada or chili rellenos, or a good piece of fresh Pacific fish. He went back to the front desk where there was now a female, a pretty Mexican, probably around twenty. He immediately flashed to his ill-fated waitress at the Mountain Kitchen, not a happy thought. Using his limited Spanish he asked her where there was a very fine restaurant where he could dine. She told him of a hotel with fine dining about a twenty minute drive from there. He decided he would go there after having a few tequila shots in his room and cleaning himself up, a little.

While he felt somewhat hung over from all that tequila he'd been guzzling, he also felt more relaxed than he had been since saying farewell to Karyn and David. He even did a brief version of "La

Bomba" in the car. Once at the Hotel, which definitely seemed a cut above the usual in Santo Rosalia, he entered the small but well appointed dining room. He was seated at the only unoccupied table and once he was given his Corona beer, started looking around the room to check out his fellow diners. They were mostly well dressed Mexicans, with one American couple at the table next to his.

After ordering *carnitas asada* with black beans and rice and another beer, Hank kept gazing around the room, doing what might be called people watching with a definite edge to it. Yes, his looking was only curiosity, but it was to find out if there was anyone in the room that he should worry about. Seeing no such person, he dug into his excellent dinner with great gusto. He topped off his meal with *flan* and a delicious cup of strong Mexican coffee. Following that up with a superb M*argarita,* Hank was now a happy camper, the best he had felt since pre-fight Ensenada, or more specifically, Kentucky Fried Chicken, where for the first time in his life he had felt like a totally contented family man. He cherished that fast-fading memory, wanting to hold onto it as long as possible.

As he was getting ready to ask for his check, Hank noticed one of the male Mexican customers going to the dining room manager who was in a white tuxedo, and whispering something in his ear. The manager's eyes darted over to Hank, and as soon as he whispered something back in the man's ear and started slowly walking toward Hank, the man got his wife and they quietly slipped out the main entrance.

When the manager got closer to him, Hank asked the man in English, "Sir, is there a problem?"

" Well, my friend, I don't know. If you will just quietly leave now with your dinner on us, there will be no problem."

"Why do you want me to leave?"

The manager reached out, gently putting his hand on Hank's back and moving him further back out of hearing range of other customers.

"*Señor*", the manager whispered, "The man who just left with his wife told me they had come back from San Diego yesterday and saw your picture in the paper, where are you are wanted for possible murder, and everyone here, including me, *Señor*, will feel better if you leave. We want no problem here, and if you go now, we will wait a few minutes before contacting the authorities. I am very sorry about this."

The manager seemed very relieved when Hank told him he fully understood and would leave immediately, which he did. Driving away as quickly as he could, he began wondering what name the newspaper used for him, but he guessed it was Hank Bellakoff, or maybe even "Hammerin' Hank Bellakoff" the name that was used when introducing him in the ring.

He had not yet thought beyond that, about what he was now going to do, where he would go, and what impact it would have on his future, etc. It's not good, he admitted to himself, to be in survival mode, which he was, and to have no idea of what you were going to do or where to go to do it, which he did...no idea...not a clue.

He suddenly remembered the tour book discussing the ferry out of Santo Rosalia to the Mexican mainland. When he got back to his room, he searched the book until he found that the ferry goes to Guaymas, Sonora, but in reading more he also learned that Sonora is the most crime-riddled state in Mexico, which for Hank was a definite no-no. The last thing he needed was to be living amongst Mexican mobsters, especially those who might have cousins in Boston.

One thing he was unsure of is whether the Mexican government would extradite him to San Diego, or just let him live in their country as an American renegade. In old cowboy movies bad guys would flee to Mexico where they could hide forever, but Hank figured that must have changed at some point, and dropped the thought.

Thinking things could be over for him soon, he decided he had nothing to lose now by calling Karyn, except maybe for Karyn herself. But he also knew he needed to talk with her at least once more. He pulled the L.A. phone number Marge had given him from his wallet, searched for and found a phone booth in a quiet location, and with some trepidation, placed the call.

David answered the phone, and as soon as he heard Hank's voice started yelling, "Mom! Mom! It's Hank, Mom, it's Hank."

He heard Karyn yelling,"Oh my God !"... and then, "Oh, Hank my love, Hank, where are you? Are you alright?"

"I'm okay for now, but I'm not sure how much longer I will be. I needed to call you to tell you how incredibly much I love you. I want to be with you and David more than anything."

"I know, Hank. I had a wonderful long talk with Marge last night. She told that if I heard from you to tell you she sends her love. Oh, Hank, please come here to me. Come home."

Those last two words immediately brought tears to his eyes. All his life his favorite song, even more so than "La Bomba" was a sad song entitled, "I'm Always Chasing Rainbows", and he knew that in Karyn he had finally found his pot of gold, his blue bird of happiness, but might never get to be with her.

"Karyn, I hope you know the murder they say I committed was the result of an accident in a fight that was self defense."

"I know that, Hank, and I know the man you are is a good man, Hank. and I'm also sure you never meant to hurt that boxer who died."

Those last words cut into Hank like a knife. Would he ever be able to tell Karyn the truth about the fight with Archie? Who knows? The more important issue is whether he will ever see her again!

"Karyn,... I don't know what else to say right now...I love you so much, and I'm afraid I'll be spending the rest of my life..."

"Running?", she interjected.

Hank paused for a moment, and then said, "Falling."

TWENTY-FOUR

HANK AND HENRY

The rest of the conversation with Karyn involved her telling him to come there, and him telling her how much he wanted to, but that it would not be a story with a happy ending, and that, he believed, was the last thing in the world he wanted to inflict on her and David. The call ended with both of them crying.

Hank had always struggled with making a woman cry, a throwback to when his mother would frequently use tears instead of anger to get him to do what she wanted. To make a woman cry, at some level for Hank, meant not being a good boy, or later, a good man.

As he started to do this kind of introspecting, something he rarely ever did in his life up to now, he realized that what he needed to do next was to go back to his room on the cliff, pack, finish off whatever tequila he had left up there, and then get out of town fast, very fast. When he approached the road up to the cliffs, he could see the Mexican cop car parked in front of the motel office, and as he saw he was too late, he got that strange combination of feelings, a sinking stomach and and an almost numb tingling throughout his body. Luckily, he had both his well stuffed wallet and his gun with him. he turned his car around and headed for the highway

As he drove south toward La Paz at the bottom of the Peninsula he knew what he needed to do was to stop at a store to buy a few bottles of tequila, find a secluded and well hidden pull-off from the highway, drink himself silly, and sleep in his car.

Dangerous? Sure, but at the moment it seemed to be exactly the right thing to do.

He found a place about twenty miles north, about three minutes off the highway, and well out of sight after he slowly nestled his car into a perfect nest of very large and dense growths of brush. He opened one the two bottles of tequila he had just bought at a small store that was pretty isolated in this small populated rural area. He was sure the old man running the place had no idea who he was. Now Hank was safely in his car, parked in the bushes, and sucking the bitter milk out of the nipple that was a Black Sombrero Tequila bottle. In less than an hour he was sound asleep.

———

Henry hadn't been himself for several days, now, and both his parents were beginning to notice. Ten year old boys are not supposed to be moody. It was his mother who finally confronted him about it.

"Henry Bellakoff, what in the world has been going on with you the past few days. You know we're all upset about Bubbie Bellakoff, but you have been acting very strangely."

Her voice had a sharpness to it he was familiar with, a reality about how his mother viewed him that would mushroom in a few years when his father would be suddenly gone, and he became her sole, unprotected target. However, on this occasion, when Henry broke into tears and explained his feelings to his mother, he got, for one of the few times in his memory a softer, warmer, nurturing response from this cold and bitter woman.

"Mom, I'm to blame for Bubbie's dying...it's my fault:"

Henry, what in the world are you talking about ? Bubbie Bellakoff died of a heart attack at her house. You're not to blame for anything about that."

"Mom, when Dad came home that night that she died, I was in bed, but I wasn't sleeping. I heard him crying when you told him about the phone call, and I knew I was to blame for making my father cry for the first time ever."

"First of all, Henry, that was not the first time your father ever cried...believe me. It was probably the first time you ever heard him cry, but not a first for him. Second, Henry, there was nothing you ever did that hurt Bubbie, let alone killed her."

"But Mom, the day she died I broke Dad's shaving mirror."

"You what? And what's that got to do with Bubbie, may she rest in peace ?"

"Remember how you and Dad have always been warning Barney and me to always stay out of your bedroom? Well, that afternoon when you were out, I snuck into your room and was playing with the things on top of the big bureau. I looked at that brush an comb that looked like ivory, I smelled a few of your little perfume bottles, and then I started playing with Dad's shaving mirror, you know, the round swivel one that's normal on one side and magnifying glass on the other. I ended up dropping it on the floor, and the normal side got a big crack all the way across it. I know I shouldn't have been in there, and I know all about how breaking a mirror brings very bad luck, and then later you got the call about Bubbie dying."

Henry's mother, with a warm smile, pulled her ten year old rascal of a boy to her, gave him a little hug, and guaranteed him that his misdeed and his seventy year old grandmother's heart attack were in no way connected. Because it was a rare thing in his youth for this woman to take him off the hook when she was usually blaming him for lots of things, Henry immediately believed her and felt very relieved. Maybe he was a bad boy that day, but definitely not a murderer.

Hank woke up squinting in the morning sun and with a horrendous headache. He also felt a stiffness throughout his body that quickly subsided once he got out of the car and peed in the bushes. Hank figured they needed watering anyway.

With creaky bones at his age, what would it be like when he was sixty or seventy? Preferring not to think about it, he got back into his car and opened the second bottle of Black Sombrero, taking a sizable swig. He swirled his Mexican Listerine around in his mouth, gargled with it, then swallowed the stuff, feeling the effects of cleaning his oral cavity with battery acid..."It really does the trick...and quick!", the TV ad would say.

What now, he wondered, as he tried to plan out the rest of the day and night ahead. It's so hard to go anywhere or do anything when your face is plastered all over creation as the face of a murderer. How can you even buy gas? Or tequila?

The idea of food had somehow on his "life's list of important things" dropped a few slots in the rankings.He knew he had to do something to change his appearance, but to do that he would have to go into a store to buy items he would need to make those changes. He searched his car for disguise aids, and found only a pair of sunglasses and a black ink marking pen he quickly used to fashion a ridiculous looking moustache/goatee combination that would only be believable for a Mexican with failing vision. He decided it was not even worth a try.

His other approach was to just go into whatever type of store he wanted, buy things quickly, and drive off even more quickly. The gasoline part proved be the biggest problem because of the time it took to get enough into his tank. Sleeping in his car was his only option for now, and he spent the next several days doing that. His diet consisted of tequila, packaged pastries and chips, fruit juices, and canned meats, fish, and veggies.At times he longed for a cheese burger, or yes, even a good steamed hot dog. He knew he was losing weight at a fairly fast clip, but that was okay, acknowledging that since he would never again box professionally, he no longer had any need to monitor weight changes with division weight limit rules in mind.

The thought of his professional boxing career being over surprised him with an immediate powerful sense of loss and grief, which he attempted to squelch with a few swigs of Black Sombrero... with little success

———

Henry sat alone, stony-faced, two spaces removed from his mother and Barney in the front row at the synagogue, as the rabbi droned on, chanting Hebrew prayers he didn't know, and didn't want to know. He was experiencing a pain, a deep pain that cut across his upper body from right shoulder to left hip. He especially experienced it in the area of his heart, where he felt pressure and a dull ache.

It was barely thirty-six hours since his father had collapsed in the dining room as he was getting up from the dinner table to get himself some Pepto Bismol from the bathroom cabinet because he was experiencing heartburn and indigestion. He was pretty much dead as he hit the floor, they were told by the medical emergency people, and he probably didn't suffer much. A half -hour later he was gone, headed to the funeral home for whatever they did to bodies there. Yesterday was the day-long viewing, although his mom insisted on a closed casket. And now today, as Jews are supposed to do, will be a brief service, a quick burial, to be followed by lots of visiting relatives, and mountains of food. So the last time he saw his father was as they took him out the door on a stretcher, covered by a sheet.

Lots of people seemed to be trying to offer support to his mother and Barney, but Henry only got the repetitive message from anyone who stopped to talk to him, that he was now the man of the family and needed to take care of his mother and little brother.Henry was equally quiet and isolated at the cemetery as he watched his father's coffin lowered into the dug hole. After the rabbi said a brief prayer, Henry followed his mother and Barney in throwing a small handful of dirt into the hole, and then stood watching two black men shoveling dirt into the hole. When the coffin was no longer visible, Henry left and went to the funeral home's black limousine, his eyes filled with tears, and his heart thumping.

As the limousine rode out of the cemetery, Henry had the thought, "If only I could see him one more time..."

———

Hank was now both depressed and drunk enough to be immobilized, but had just enough functionality to buy some gas, Black Sombrero, and packages of the same ridiculous food from a store owner he was sure recognized him and who probably called the cops immediately after he left. Once again, he found a turn-off suitable for a night's shelter.

He now had a pretty constant headache, a growling stomach, and a craving for a real toilet and a shower. He realized he was in a downward spiral, and with no foreseeable way of bringing it to a halt. As he had that thought, he could see his whole body shaking slightly, a visible sign that he was scared to death,...almost literally. But Hank also became aware of that other feeling, the big one that had plagued him for most of his life,... the one that made everything so much worse. It was that feeling ...that knowing... that he was alone. At that moment of awareness, Hank lay down across his front seat, his head next to the passenger's door, drew his knees up toward his chest, and folded his arms together tightly against his chest ... scared ...alone... vulnerable. He easily could have fallen asleep in that universal fetal position, but he sprang up into the driver's seat when a bright light was shining in the vicinity of his car.

Hank silently cursed at the misfortune that this turn-off location was no longer safe. He peered out of his window toward the light, but it went out just as he did. While the moonlight wasn't quite strong enough to illuminate this diabolical intrusion, his ears told him everything he needed to know. A couple of what sounded like young Mexicans of the *hombre'- mujer* variety had parked their car, turned off their lights, popped open some beer, and went through several minutes of alternating periods of giggling and heavy breathing. Hank felt himself smiling for the first time in days, but started up his car, knowing he would to find another place to spend the night. He sped out of his hide-away heading back toward the highway. He probably scared those kids to death with the noise he made.

Now what?" he yelled out to some imaginary audience, as he drove north...north again...to where? To what? To who?

Hank felt totally spent at this point, and in the absence of any cognitive clarity, he simply headed back toward his last home away from home, the motel on the cliff.

As he got close to the cliffs area, Hank looked around and saw no lights on. There had been many vacancies when he was there before, and as he pulled up next to the back of the motel, it seemed that way now. He thought the cops would be very unlikely to look at him up there, and so he sighed, hunkered down into his seat, sucking out the last few drops from his next to last bottle of Black Sombrero, then cursing and tossing the empty out his window, he opened up his last one, taking an immediate burning swig. He felt an immediate urge to look for a phone booth so he could call Bubba. He missed Bubba more than anyone, and felt he needed to talk with him. Before he got any further with this impulse, he stopped himself, reminding his weary mind that Bubba's jaw was still wired shut, and would not be able to use the phone. Hank slumped back into his seat.

Once again he started to drift off just as earlier, before being rudely interrupted by the horny young couple. He fell into a not very deep sleep (too scared for such a luxury), and soon images of many people from his recent life were flashing before him...Bubba, and Donna, and Karyn, and Charlie Schumacher, and Bev, and Doc, and Susie, and even Molly the Round Cards girl, So many images...and all of them were leading the sleeping Hank into wondering how in hell he ever got to where he was now...how had he fallen so far?

Hank woke up out of that half sleep state, this time the intruder being his intense need to empty his bladder. He got out of his car, preparing to pee on the back wall of this great Mexican resort hotel, where there was no extra charge for the bed bugs, when he was hit with a recollection that made him smile for the second time tonight. It was of his dad at the beach. Whenever he had to pee, he would go into the water, facing the ocean, only up to his ankles if no one was around, deeper if anyone was, place a fist on each of his hips, and then let it flow, into God's vast salt water pool. People in the family always knew when his dad was peeing in the ocean, but no one else ever did. It was sort of a family joke. One time, when his dad went out into deeper, more concealing water, he remembered asking him why he did that, and his dad answered with a wry smile on his face, "It's windy today...too much blowback."

That last recollection made Hank laugh out loud, and he immediately turned, facing the sea of Cortez, went to cliff's edge, opened his fly, placed his fists on his hips, and let his bladder's reservoir of tequila-infused urine flow freely into the night.

God, that felt good, he thought, and stood there for a few minutes, savoring the moment.

As he turned to walk back to his car, Hank accidentally stepped on the empty Black Sombrero bottle, and fell to the ground, and then his body rolled several times up to and then over the edge of the cliff. As he was falling face down toward the sea, the last thing he saw was a lone man in a royal blue bathing suit illuminated by moonlight, standing knee deep in the water, arms outstretched, preparing to catch him.

THE END

TWENTY-FIVE

EPILOGUE

BACK IN THE RING

H ank was wearing the luxuriously thick blue and white hooded terry cloth robe he always wore when he fought. It felt so good to have it on once again. He stood alone in the middle of an empty ring in an equally empty but well lighted arena. He had just come in himself, and he had been very impressed with the outside fluorescent marquee that had emblazoned on it the words:

"FEATURED ATTRACTION TONIGHT"
"HENRY HAMMERIN' HANK BELLAKOFF"

He stood alone in the center of the ring for several minutes, wondering what would be happening next. Then he heard a large stadium door open and close, and he saw a single male figure walking toward the ring. He wondered if the Boston mob had finally caught up with him, albeit a little too late. But the man, who entered the ring through the ropes was a man wearing a gold tuxedo jacket, black pants and shoes, and a sparkling white shirt and black bow tie, much like Michael Buffer, the world famous ring announcer. Hank had met

Michael several times when his fight was on TV. He was a little narcissistic, surprise, surprise, but also a really nice guy. All the women in the boxing world certainly gravitated toward this strikingly handsome man. But it was not Michael Buffer. It was Hank's dad, resplendent in the Buffer-like outfit.

"Hi, Dad", Hank said,

His dad just nodded and smiled. As he did, two large arena doors opened, one at either end of the building, and people started coming in and then down to claim their ringside seats for this special occasion.

Hank's dad stepped forward, microphone in hand, and welcomed everyone to the evening's main event as, "One big round of talking, for the currently partially vacant *Understanding One`s Life Anyweight Crown.* So ladies and gentlemen, *madames and monsieurs,* LET`S GET READY TO RUMBLE! Introducing our main gladiator, a man who fought the good fight and tried to have a good life, and who now needs to learn more about what it was all about. My son, Henry Hammerin' Hank Belllllakoff!"

The way the name Bellakoff rolled off his tongue in grand Buffer-esque eloquence brought smiles to both Hank's and his dad's faces.

As the gathered ringside crowd cheered, Hank could hear a few strong "boos" mixed in. He started to look around the crowd to see who was there. It was an amazing array of people from various parts of his life, especially childhood and the recent past. He could see in the now somewhat lowered arena lights Bubba, and Bev, and Terry, and Marge, and Doc, and Susie, and Charlie, and Cousin Janette and Aunt Naomi, and Donna (who, he couldn't help but notice, was sitting with Jack), and Karyn and David, and Barney and his mother, and the manager at the Mexican hotel restaurant, with some other Mexican guy he didn't recognize. He even saw Archie and Jack, his two victims, who were sitting together off to the side.

Before he could begin to speak, a bell rang and a rounds card girl came out with a big number one card, flashing it to the crowd with a sexy little swing of her hips. It was Molly, who spoke to him as she was leaving the ring. "By the way, I never met you, but the bartender at the Sham told me you wanted to look me up. I wish you did. I always had a wicked crush on you, and I would have done anything you wanted if I could have been with you, and your life might have gone better than it did. Sorry."

Hank debated whether or not to tell her he did look for her and found her, but decided not to pursue her. Was she right? Would his life have been better if he had? Her expression, "wicked crush" had teen-ager written all over it, not really his cup of tea, and he ended up saying nothing to her as she bent down and slipped through the ropes, out of the ring and out of the big arena to the world beyond.

Hank's father handed him the microphone and stepped back from his son and the spotlight. Hank just stood there in silence for a moment, and then a very familiar voice broke in.

"Hey, kid, how are you doin'?" It was Bubba, good old Bubba, not wired at the jaw, and looking pretty good.

"Obviously not very well", Hank answered, and the audience reacted with warm, good-natured laughter.

"Yeah, Hank, I thought for sure I'd go before you, but I guess not. I felt horrible about the news."

"Thanks, Bub. You know I really loved you, sort of like a father figure."

Hank's father felt good hearing he was that important to his son, and called out a quiet "Sorry I left you, Henry. I really had no choice."

"Yeah, thanks, kid, I loved you, too." Bubba replied.

"Hank, daaahling," Bev called up to him with a mock Tallulah Bankhead accent, as she rose from her second row seat. Hank couldn't help but notice she had been seated between Charlie Schumacher and Doc Luchesa, a rather curious threesome.

"Hello, Bev." Hank could feel the anxiety in his voice, and he figured Bev did also.

"Relax, big boy, I don't bite."

There was a flippancy bordering on taunting in her usually velvety voice, and Hank could feel himself starting to sweat in the cool arena.

"I just wanted to set the record straight about a few things. One is that I really did have some great times with you during our relationship, and I really did care for you, so don't ever doubt that. But, sweet guy, you never really figured out an important part of who I am, and I think maybe I was trying to hide it from you, because I knew you wouldn't be able to handle the situation. You are such a nice guy, Hank, that I began to find it boring, not stimulating enough. I'm like lots of other women, Hank, I'm drawn to danger, maybe even to bad guys who aren't so nice. I thought you might have noticed when we'd see movies that had that dynamic in it, or when you'd introduce me to some of the less savory characters in the boxing world. But you never did pick up on that. Maybe even a little angry jealousy would have stirred up the pot a little. But, it's too late now."

Bev continued, "I also wanted you to know that I got Charlie to go easy with you about your thing with Archie. He and I are living together now since he left his wife last year. We both talked Doc into not sending anyone out to kill you, but it appears you found your own way to off yourself. We're sorry it turned out that way, but you know that old song, 'Only The Good Die Young.' Happy eternity, sweet boy, and I'm glad you found your father."

As Bev sat back down, Hank thought he saw her wipe a few tears from under her eyes, but then told himself he was probably just being that same old wishful romantic he'd been his whole life, chasing rainbows. She was probably happy with "old Mr. Potter", who certainly wasn't "nice."

Hank barely had time to take a deep breath and push away his hurt feelings, when Marge got up and told him that she thought he was the nicest man she ever met, and that if she was fifteen years younger she would have chased his ass all over San Diego and tried to get him to marry her.

At that point Terry stood up and said, "Hank, you really are a great guy, and everything that happened that night was very real for me just as I know it was for you. I am so very sorry I didn't tell you about Jack. I was pretty sure that would make you back off, and I wanted to be with you so bad. I'm really glad I got to be with you, Hank, no regrets on my part."

As Hank smiled back at her and nodded his appreciation of her words, he could see that Terry didn't have a mark on her, and that Jack must have taken out all his rage on that poor young waitress,... and on Hank himself. It was likely that beautiful, sexual Terry was the dominant person in that marriage, he thought.

Susie was next, and not surprisingly told him he made a big mistake by not pursuing her, and also that she was sad about his "departure."

Jack Toohey rose very slowly from his seat next to Donna, whom Hank had been avoiding looking at, and said "Hank, I've debated whether to say anything tonight, but I guess I will. I was really glad to see you were dead, because it meant I could finally let go of my feelings about wanting to kill you myself. There were times when Doc talked me out of it, telling me he would get some people to do it, but somewhere down the road. Well, Hank, I'm glad your road has dead ended. You messed with my wife and tried to steal her from me, TWICE!"

Jack was now red in the face, and Donna was tugging on his sport coat to try to get him to sit down, but he wouldn't.

"Lucky for me, she came to her senses both times, although I did have to lean on her pretty hard the second time. I told her if she went out that door I would kill both of you, and if she stayed, I would get some friends to beat the shit out of you, but not kill you. She got the point and decided to stay, and I think she's glad she did, right Baby?" Jack was now looking at Donna, who couldn't look up and look at Hank, at all.

"Yeah Jack, I'm glad. Now please sit down."

Jack did as she asked.

So, Hank thought to himself, Doc Luchesa was the head of the mob in Boston, and Donna really was planning to go with him until Jack found out, at least it appeared that way. He would have loved a chance to talk about all this with Donna, but he knew he would never get that chance...ever.

Hank felt a stabbing pain in his chest as Karyn stood up, crying. He wanted so much to run to her and hold her, but knew he couldn't.

"Hank, my darling Hank, I loved you so much, and so did David. I was so hurt and sad when you wouldn't join us in Los Angeles. You should have come to us. Somehow we would have gotten through all of it, and had the kind of life together we both wanted. What a waste of life, Hank, and you believed you were doing the right thing to protect David and me. just like you told me you used to do for your mother and brother. Oh, Hank, can't you see that you get trapped in good boy stuff and end up not taking care of yourself? Everybody loses this way, and it shouldn't have been your story because you were a good, kind, loving man, the best I've ever known."

Archie rose quickly and yelled out, "You're delusional lady. This guy was a sneaky, mean, cheating son-of-a-bitch, and he killed me, and this fella' Jack sitting next to me, and you people still call him a good man? Bullshit!"

Archie and Jack Slocum then stormed out of the arena, back to wherever it was they came from.

"I don't care what he says, Hank, you are a good man, and I love you so much, and I want you to come back." It was David, with lots of tears, and obviously a child's struggles understanding and accepting the grim realities of death.

Karyn was hugging David as Barney stood up, nervously clearing his throat, and saying something Hank had never heard before.

"Hank, you were a good brother to me, trying to be like Dad and doing your best to take care of Mom and me. We will never forget you, and God bless you."

Hank's mother looked up for a moment and, as usual, was having a variety of feelings. Hank was glad she never spoke.

And then the stranger who had come in with the restaurant

manager stood and and said, "Hello, Hank, my name is Carlos Morales, and I am the coroner for Central Baja California." The well dressed middle-aged Mexican man continued, "I came here tonight not to tell you anything, but to ask you a few questions."

"Shoot !", said Hank.

"Okay, thank you for your cooperation. You probably know we found your body washed up onto the little strip of beach at water's edge. You obviously had fallen off the cliff above, and I also must say that your blood alcohol level...well let's just say you were higher than the cliffs when you fell."

"Yeah, I was," Hank responded, a little sheepishly. "That Black Sombrero Tequila packs quite a wallop."

"Yes it does," Morales continued. "So when we went up to the area from which you fell, at the motel you had stayed at, we saw a few tequila bottles up there, and wondered if you may have tripped on one them, rather than just passing out. Is that what happened?"

"Actually, that is what happened. Good job Mr. Morales"

"And then we figured from where the bottles were, and from the scuff marks on the ground, that you must have hit the ground a few feet from the edge, but then your body must have rolled a little for you to go over the edge."

"*Señor Morales,* you do your job very well," Hank affirmed.

"So, Mr. Bellakoff, Hank, that leaves me with the last big question I have for you. When you rolled over the edge, was it an accident, or did you do it on purpose?"

Hank suddenly felt numb all over, and he was alone in the ring in the now empty well-lighted arena. Just Hank and the Morales question remained. Hank stood motionless for many minutes, his mind struggling and swirling like never before.

Then he climbed out of the ring, walked to the back of the arena, and turned off all the lights. Hank stood in the darkness for a while, and then opened an arena door, and went out into the darkness that lay beyond.

———

For My Father And For My Sons.

Dear reader,

We hope you enjoyed reading *Falling*. Please take a moment to leave a review in Amazon, even if it's a short one. Your opinion is important to us.

Discover more books by Ralph Zieff at https://www.nextchapter. pub/authors/ralph-zieff

Want to know when one of our books is free or discounted for Kindle? Join the newsletter at http://eepurl.com/bqqB3H

Best regards,

Ralph Zieff and the Next Chapter Team

You might also like:
Willard Notch by Ralph Zieff

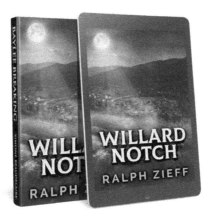

To read the first chapter for free, please head to:
https://www.nextchapter.pub/books/willard-notch

Lightning Source UK Ltd.
Milton Keynes UK
UKHW010749100920
369682UK00001B/239